AREA 51

BY
ROBIN MOORE

To Mank Collins—

John Moore

KINGFISHER
An imprint of Larousse plc
Elsley House
24–30 Great Titchfield Street
London W1P 7AD

Copyright © Larousse plc 1997
Text copyright © Robin Moore 1997

First published by Larousse plc 1997

10 9 8 7 6 5 4 3

A CIP catalogue record for this book is available from the British Library

ISBN 0 7534 0138 X

"You will have to make your own minds up about how many of the 'facts' contained in this story are true. Some are based on public information, but others are the result of a fictional interpretation by the author of events, what might have been said or done. Some names have been changed, as you can see, to protect the individuals involved."

Designed and typeset by Tracey McNerney
Printed in the United Kingdom

Contents Page

Introduction   page iv

Chapter One   page 1

Chapter Two   page 7

Chapter Three   page 10

Chapter Four   page 17

Chapter Five   page 22

Chapter Six   page 31

Chapter Seven   page 38

Chapter Eight   page 43

Chapter Nine   page 49

Chapter Ten   page 60

Chapter Eleven   page 70

Afterword   page 75

Glossary   page 77

Biographies   page 80

Classified Files   page 82

Introduction

In a remote corner of the Nevada desert, hidden behind a range of sharp-peaked mountains, lies an air base so secret it doesn't appear on any map. Insiders call it Area 51. This restricted area is larger than the states of Connecticut and Rhode Island combined and has the longest runway in the world. There, under a cloak of Government secrecy, the US Military tests its most advanced aircraft.

Meanwhile, less than fifty kilometres away, just outside the small desert town of Rachel, Nevada, people come from all over the world to gather at a weather-beaten black mailbox along State Highway 375.

From this vantage point, observers say they have seen brightly lit objects flying over the base, objects which appear to defy the laws of gravity.

Because the test facility is funded by a 'black budget' that not even the most high-ranking members of Congress are permitted to review, the truth about what really goes on in Area 51 has been hidden away, in files that most people never get to see. Files marked:

CLASSIFIED

CHAPTER ONE

Like most test pilots in the US Air Force, Major Daniel Hawkins thought he was indestructible.

Somehow, he had survived everything life had thrown at him. He had flown long-range reconnaissance missions in Vietnam and Cambodia. He had crash-landed in the mountains of Thailand and been shot down over the South China Sea. He had flown through hailstorms and blizzards and tropical hurricanes.

But, up until today, he had never even come close to hitting a cow.

It was late in the afternoon on July 7, 1988. Major Hawkins was driving through a remote section of the Nevada desert, heading for his new duty station. He had just bought a fire-red Camaro and had driven all the way from Florida, stopping only to eat and catch a few hours' sleep at his sister's place in Texas. The long hours of driving with the top down and the wind tearing at his hair made Hawkins feel light and free and knife-edge alive.

The open range slipped by in a blur. It was a vast emptiness, dotted with cactus and sagebrush, bordered by rugged ranges of treeless mountains, scorched brown by the Sun. Every now and then, a rusted watering trough or a rancher's dilapidated windmill showed among the foothills. Otherwise, there were no signs of human habitation.

Hawkins removed his sunglasses and wiped the sweat from his eyes with the back of his hand. He eased up on the accelerator, squinting through the grime-covered windscreen.

There was something up ahead, on the highway. In the shimmering heat that danced off the blacktop, he could see a mass of indistinct shapes, moving around on the road.

Hawkins flicked his eyes down to the speedometer. He

was cruising at 120 kilometres an hour. Quickly, he glanced to the left and right. But there were no side roads, not even a decent pull-over lane.

Hawkins began pumping the brake. He leaned on the horn.

Then, when he was less than a hundred metres away, he saw them clearly: a dozen sleepy-eyed, cud-chewing cows, standing in the middle of the road, as big as life. One was even lying down staring straight back at him.

At the last moment, when he was almost on top of them, Hawkins jerked the wheel to the right and plunged off the road.The Camaro bucked and bounced like a wild mustang, ploughing through the cactus and sagebrush, kicking up a huge cloud of dust. Hawkins couldn't see a thing. He struggled to hold the wheel steady.

Suddenly, the car pitched forward and dropped over a steep embankment. For a few terrifying seconds, Hawkins thought it was going to flip over. Then he heard the sound of crumpling metal and the car ground to a halt, nose-down in an erosion ditch.

As the dust cleared, Hawkins fumbled with the latch of his seat belt. His head felt like a pumpkin, as if he had just awakened after a long night of celebrating at the officers' club. He looked up and caught a glimpse of himself in the rearview mirror. His nose was bleeding and he had a nasty cut over his left eye. Otherwise, he seemed unharmed.

Hawkins looked around. The Camaro was demolished. The bonnet was buried in a pile of gravel and the windscreen was a spider's web of shattered glass. Hawkins climbed out of the car and crawled up out of the ditch on his hands and knees. When he reached level ground, he sat down on a big rock and stripped off his t-shirt so he could wipe the blood out of his eyes.

For a few moments, the desert was eerily quiet. The only sound was the mooing of the cows, milling around on the highway.

Then Hawkins heard a vehicle approaching. He turned and saw an old, rusting pick-up truck turn off the road and bounce across the open range in his direction. The truck pulled up just ahead of him and rolled to a stop.

Hawkins noticed a faded bumper sticker plastered across the back bumper which read:

'I Will Give Up My Gun When They Pry My Cold, Dead Finger From The Trigger.'

He had scarcely finished reading when he heard the truck door slam and saw a wiry figure, wearing a weather-beaten cowboy hat and carrying a pump-action deer rifle, come limping towards him.

"I hope you've got insurance," the rancher said.

Hawkins peered up into the ancient face under the hat-brim.

"You're a woman," he said in surprise.

"Yeah," the old woman said, "and you're a lousy driver."

Her face was as rugged as the desert itself, as lined and creased as a lizard's skin.

She was dressed in dusty denim work clothes and wore a scuffed pair of snakeskin cowboy boots.

"I don't like to see my cattle frightened like that," she said sourly.

Hawkins spat a mouthful of blood out on to the ground.

He was about to give her a piece of his mind but there was something about the way she carried the rifle, with her wrinkled finger casually wrapped around the trigger, that made him reconsider.

"Listen, Ma'am," he said at last, "your cows were standing *right* in the middle of the road."

"That's right," the old woman said, "we got tan ones for the day and black ones for the night. You gotta keep your eye out for 'em! What's wrong with you? Don't they have cattle where you're from?"

"Well, of course we do," Hawkins said, "but we don't let them wander all over the roadways! Didn't you ever hear of fences?"

The old woman threw back her head and laughed. She sounded like a coyote, howling at the Moon.

"Fences?" she hollered. "What do we need fences for? Sonny, this is the wild west. We got more cattle out here than people. It's the people we oughta put behind fences!"

Hawkins got to his feet, still holding the bloody shirt to his forehead. He kept his eyes on her gun hand. He certainly didn't want to frighten her. There was no telling what the old woman might do if he made the wrong move. After all the action he had seen, he had no intention of being shot by a crazy old women over a bunch of cows.

"Listen, Ma'am," he said, "this is all very interesting, but I'm not in the mood for a philosophical discussion right now. Could you do me a favour and give me a ride in to town?"

"Ain't no town anywheres near here," she said, "unless you count Rachel. But that ain't a town really, just a few trailers, a gas station and a roadside diner."

Suddenly, the woman stopped as if she had just thought of something. Her eyes narrowed.

"Say," she said slowly, "you ain't one of those 'saucer nuts' are you?"

"What?"

"You know, the Black Mailbox and all that?"

"Ma'am, I don't have the foggiest idea what you're talking about."

She shook her head in disgust.

"You don't know anythin', do you?" she said. "Don't you *know* where you're at? You're in flyin' saucer country, boy! We get UFO goofballs from all over the world. They drive up here from Vegas and set out along the highway at night, near Steve Medlin's mailbox. They say they see flyin' saucers zippin' around over the air base – oh, excuse me – the secret air base.

"I know, I know. The whole danged facility is supposed to be a *big* secret. But after forty years of livin' next-door to a top-secret nonexistent air base, the novelty has done wore off. The way I figure it, there's only two kinda strangers that show up around here: saucer nuts and military. If you're not the UFO type, then you gotta be military."

Hawkins just stared at her. He didn't have any intention of discussing the air base with her. After all, that was classified information. Actually, he didn't have much to tell. Hawkins had been told very little about his new assignment. All he knew was that he would be testing some of the Air Force's most advanced aircraft.

Hawkins mopped the blood from above his left eye, trying to look pitiful. He thought the messiness of his head wound might gain him some sympathy.

"All right," she said at last, slapping the dust from her pants' leg, "don't just stand there bleedin' all over my ground. Get in the truck and I'll take you up to Rachel. There's a pay phone at the gas station. You can make some calls and get somebody out here to tow this motor of yours off my land. And don't forget to give me that insurance information!"

Hawkins shook his head and started to walk toward the truck.

"What you *seem* to forget," he reminded her, "is that I missed your cows. What kind of damages are you going to claim?"

"I don't rightly know," she said, "but I'll think of somethin'."

Hawkins pulled open the truck door on the passenger's side and climbed in. The inside of the truck was filthy. The cloth seats and metal dashboard were covered with a thick layer of powdery desert dust. The floor was littered with yellowed sheets of newspaper, musty-smelling burlap sacks and crushed soda cans. But he tried to keep his blood to himself all the same.

The old woman placed her rifle on the overhead rack then turned to face him. She looked at his swelling forehead and bloody hands. Through the streaks of red, she noticed the blue pilot's wings tattooed on the back of his left hand.

"So you're a flyboy, huh?" she asked.

When Hawkins didn't answer, she just shook her head.

"No sense playin' dumb with me," she said, "I know your kind. My husband was a pilot. Flew Black Widows durin' the War. Ran off with some Vegas woman back in the 60s. Left me with a tumbled-down ranch to run and five kids to raise. I been in a bad mood ever since."

"I'm sorry to hear that," Hawkins said.

"Don't be. I wouldn't give a wooden nickel to be married again. You know what they say: 'Love may be blind, but marriage is a great eye-opener'."

The old woman started the truck and put it in low gear, backing away from the ditch. The cab of the truck smelled of motor oil and burnt rubber. She did a three-point turn and bumped up on to the highway. By now, the cows had wandered out across the range, grazing on sage and bunch-grass. The view before them looked like a picture postcard scene of the desert at its best.

The old woman gunned the engine and headed north, towards Rachel.

CHAPTER TWO

They had been driving for less than ten minutes when the old woman pointed into the distance. "That's the Groom Mountain Range over there to the west," she said. "The air base is in a valley beyond them mountains. If you get close enough to them foothills you'll see Government signs everywhere. I've seen those signs up close and I know what they say: *'Deadly Force Is Authorized.'* That means they can shoot first and ask questions later."

They continued their journey for a while in silence. Hawkins felt his head wound start to throb. Then breaking the silence, the old woman began to talk again. But this time the hard edge was gone from her voice.

"I seen the air base once," she said quietly. "Me and my youngest boy, Duane, snuck up to the top of the Groom Range one Hallowe'en night, years ago.

"We set up there and watched the crazy lights comin' and goin' over the valley. Your pals was playin' war games, I guess. Flyin' their secret aircraft and such. I swear, if I didn't know better, I'd say those UFO people were right.

"There was some strange lights that night – bluish and purplish lights. Lights that zipped around, makin' little jerky movements. They'd come tearin' along, then stop in mid-air. Then they'd streak off again, in a totally different direction. I swear, it was like watchin' one of them special-effects shows on the TV. Only difference was, this was no TV show, it was the real thing."

Hawkins didn't reply. She was probably just a crazy old woman anyway. They travelled the rest of the way in silence.

It was almost dark when they spotted the lights of the small town of Rachel. The old woman rolled up on to the gravel parking lot in front of a place called the Roadkill

Diner.

The Roadkill was obviously the hub of social life in Rachel and, from the looks of things, the proprietors were not shy about letting everyone know it. Outside, Hawkins could see a large neon sign. The name of the diner flashed off and on, casting a strange blue light across the parking lot. Near the front door of the establishment were two smaller, hand-painted signs.

One read, *'Next time you're hungry, think of the Roadkill. You kill 'em – We'll grill 'em.'*

It showed a picture of a dead cow, with its hooves sticking up, resting on a large platter.

The other: *'Hot and Tender – Right off the Fender!'*

Hawkins realized it was going to take a while for him to get used to the local sense of humour.

The old woman was right, it wasn't much of a town. But he could see a pay phone outside the gas station, and that was encouraging.

Hawkins found a piece of cardboard and a stub of a pencil on the floor of the truck. The old woman turned on the dome light. Hawkins copied his insurance information from the card in his wallet.

When he had finished, the old woman handed him a scrap of paper with her name and address printed on it. Hawkins slipped out of the truck and closed the door behind him. It squeaked on its rusty hinges.

"Thanks for the ride," he said through the open window. "I'll get somebody out there in the next couple of days to tow my auto away."

"See that you do," the old woman said.

Then she put the truck in gear and roared off down the highway. Hawkins stood there, holding the scrap of paper in his hand. Across the top, in neat black letters, he saw the words, *The Circle S Ranch, Rachel, Nevada. Mandy Thompson, Proprietor.*

He folded the piece of paper and tucked it into his wallet.

Then he crossed the highway and walked to the pay phone.

He dialled the phone number he had been given with his travel orders.

It rang only once. A clipped voice answered.

"Security."

"This is Major Daniel Hawkins. I am scheduled to report for duty at your location this evening. But I've had some vehicular trouble and managed to get a ride as far as Rachel. Would it be possible to send a transport out to pick me up?"

"Stand by," the voice said. A few seconds later, Hawkins heard a click and another voice came on the line.

"Headquarters."

"Yes. This is Major Daniel Hawkins. I am scheduled to report to the base tonight. My auto broke down and I am stranded here in Rachel. Can you send a driver out to pick me up?"

"Of course, Sir. Could I trouble you for your serial number?"

Hawkins gave it to him. There was a delay of several moments while the orderly checked the records. Then he was back on the line.

"Very well, Sir. We'll have a driver there to pick you up in about ten minutes."

"Thanks."

Hawkins hung up and walked out under the clear sky. The first stars had begun to appear. He was able to pick out a few of the most familiar constellations.

Suddenly, far overhead, a bluish light zipped by, then vanished.

Chapter Three

Hawkins caught his first glimpse of the air base just after dark. For twenty minutes, his driver had been following a dirt road which wound steeply up a narrow mountain pass between two sharp-edged peaks. Then, suddenly, they reached the high ground and came through on the other side.

The Moon was up and Hawkins could see the secret installation down in the valley, far below. It was like a small city, rimmed by steep mountains on all sides, cradled like a bed of glowing embers on the shores of a dry lake bed.

As the vehicle wound down the mountainside, through a series of steep switchbacks and hairpin turns, Hawkins could make out the shapes of hangars and fuel tanks and satellite dishes. Arrowing across the lake bed, gleaming in the moonlight, he could see a very long runway. Next to it stood a control tower which shone like a brilliantly-illuminated insect.

The mountains on the far side of the valley were dusted with snow, making the base look stark and otherworldly, like an outpost on the Moon.

The escort immediately took him to the infirmary, where a heavy-set, stern-faced nurse cleaned and dressed his head wound. Then he was driven to another part of the compound and ushered into a dormitory-style room in one of the flat-topped buildings. Moments later, without even bothering to undress, Hawkins climbed into his bunk and fell fast asleep.

His first night in Area 51 passed without incident. When he woke in the morning, he found a security guard, dressed in camouflage fatigues and wearing a .38 calibre pistol on his hip, sitting outside the door.

The guard took one look at him and pointed down the hallway.

"Shower's in there, Major. You best get cleaned up. You've got a briefing with the Project Director at 0900 hours."

The pilot glanced at his watch. He had less than an hour to pull himself together. It wasn't until he got out of his clothes and into the shower that Hawkins realized how many cuts and bruises he had received during the crash. But he could see that they were minor injuries. Within a few days, he knew he would be back in top physical condition.

When Hawkins returned to his room, the guard was still seated by the door. Someone had left a stack of clothing and other items on his bunk. In a neatly folded pile, he found clean underwear and socks, a set of dark green Air Force fatigues, a zippered jumpsuit, a set of black leather flight boots, and a cloth bag full of toiletries.

It felt good to set aside his blood-stained civilian clothes and climb into a fresh military uniform. He returned to the bathroom, shaved and ran a comb through his hair. Hawkins stared at his image in the mirror. Except for the white bandage over his left eye, he looked fit and ready for duty.

After a quick breakfast in the nearly empty dining hall, the guard took him to a small briefing room in the complex near his quarters.

When Hawkins walked into the room, he saw a distinguished-looking officer seated behind a table, leafing through a thick file with Hawkins's name stencilled across it.

Hawkins came to attention and saluted.

"Major Daniel Hawkins, reporting for duty, Sir."

The officer returned his salute. Hawkins could tell by glancing at his uniform that he was saluting a pilot who had been heavily decorated in three wars.

"My name is Lieutenant Colonel Sheridan," the older man said. "I will be your immediate superior for the duration of your time here at the test facility."

"I have been reading through your file," he said. "Your previous commanding officer gave you a glowing recommendation. I am confident that your performance here at the Nevada Test Site will reflect the highest traditions of the United States Air Force."

"I'll do my best, Sir."

"I know you will, Major. But before we can get into the particulars of your assignment, we have a few preliminary procedures we must complete. Because the project you will be working on is of a highly sensitive nature, I must ask you to read and sign this document."

The Colonel opened the file and passed a stack of papers across the table.

"You may take a seat, Major."

The guard, who was still standing by the door, brought over a folding metal chair and seated Hawkins across the table from his superior.

The document consisted of twelve legal-size pages of closely spaced type. It took Hawkins several minutes to read. Basically, it said that if he divulged any classified information about the project or the test facility to any unauthorized person, he could receive a minimum of ten years' imprisonment and a $10,000 fine. The document went on to say that more serious breaches of security would result in the severest consequences imaginable. By signing this agreement, Hawkins understood that he was pledging to keep the details of his life in Area 51 a secret for as long as he was alive.

Hawkins signed the document and passed it back to the Colonel. He had no problem with making such a pledge. After twenty years in the Air Force, he had no intention of betraying his comrades or his country.

Colonel Sheridan studied Hawkins's signature for a moment. Then he signed his own name and placed the papers carefully into the folder.

"Please understand that the stringency of our security

measures is absolutely essential to the success of our operation," Sheridan said. "In the days and weeks ahead, you will learn many astonishing secrets.

"Even the most high-ranking members of Congress are not permitted access to some of this information. Even the President of the United States has not seen *all* of what you will see. These matters require the utmost secrecy. Do I make myself understood?"

"Yes Sir," he answered.

Hawkins stared into the Colonel's eyes. They were hard and still and gunmetal gray.

Colonel Sheridan returned to the file that lay open before him.

"I see that you have a degree in Aeronautical Design from the Air Force Academy."

"Yes Sir."

"That's what we need. You may think that you were sent here because of your flying abilities. Actually, Major, hot-shot pilots are a dime a dozen. We do need a skilful pilot who can fly our craft. But we also need someone who can interface with the scientists, talk their language. Do you understand, Hawkins?"

"Of course, Sir."

"By the way, Major, do you have any idea of the nature of this assignment?"

"No, Sir. I just assumed I would be testing some form of advanced aircraft."

The Colonel allowed himself a chuckle.

"That you will, son. That you will. Very well. Please remove your shirt, Major."

It was an unusual request, but Hawkins didn't hesitate to comply. Sheridan nodded to the guard. Hawkins heard the door open behind him.

A moment later, two medical technicians in white lab coats entered the room. Each carried a metal tray stacked with small cutting implements and vials of dark-coloured liquid.

Without the slightest introduction, the medical team swabbed down his back then took up their cutting tools and began making a patchwork of small incisions on his back. They worked quickly and efficiently, without saying a word. Hawkins winced as they began painting the open wounds with a variety of substances from the vials.

"Allergy testing," Colonel Sheridan explained. "You will be working with some unusual substances here and we want to make sure you don't have any adverse reactions."

The allergy testing took a full hour. Then the technicians wiped down his back and bandaged his cuts. "I'm starting to feel a little like a human pin cushion," Hawkins joked.

But no one laughed.

Just then, the door opened and a tall black man in an Air Force flight suit walked in.

Sheridan nodded.

"Thank you for joining us, Major Comstock. I'd like you to meet Major Hawkins.

"Daniel Hawkins, Charlie Comstock. You two will be working very closely with each other in the days ahead. I am sure you will be a good team."

Hawkins stood and shook Comstock's hand.

"Good to meet you, Major. My friends call me Danny."

Comstock smiled. "All right, Danny. I hear you graduated from the Air Force Academy. What year?"

"Class of '71."

"Is *that* so? I was there in '73. I guess we just missed each other."

Hawkins smiled, "I guess so."

"Listen, gentlemen," Sheridan said. "I have another meeting to attend. Why don't you two go over to the officers' club and shoot the breeze for a while, then have some lunch? I'll meet you back here at 1300 hours and we'll lay out our schedule for the next couple of days."

Comstock nodded.

"Sounds good to me, Sir. I'll have him back here in a few

hours."

The Colonel stood. Hawkins and Comstock snapped to attention and saluted.

"That will be all, gentlemen," the Colonel said.

The guard opened the door and waited until Hawkins and Comstock had stepped outside, then continued to walk about ten yards behind them as they headed down the street.

"Do they always shadow you like this?" Hawkins asked.

"You don't know the half of it, Danny boy. They even follow you into the bathroom around here."

Hawkins glanced back over his shoulder. It occurred to him that the security guard had a face like a bulldog.

"How long have you been here, Charlie?"

"Three days, man. They've been waiting for you to get in so they could pair us up and put us to work."

Hawkins nodded. "Do you have any idea what kind of craft we're going to be flying?"

"They haven't told me a thing. All I know is the little bit of information I've overheard."

"What was that?"

"I heard they brought us here to replace two dead pilots."

"They crashed?"

"Crashed and burned, man."

"Who told you this?"

"It's just like I said, nobody told me a thing. I overheard two of the guards talking about it. When they saw me walk up, they quit talking."

"Crashed and burned, huh?"

"Yeah."

"Not a very good omen, Charlie."

"You believe in omens?" he asked.

Hawkins smiled. "I believe in staying alive."

Comstock clapped him on the back. He had a deep, comforting way of laughing.

"That's my man," he said. "I think this is gonna be the

beginning of a very good partnership. Listen, the way I look at it, I don't want them to tell me more than I gotta know. Anything extra is only gonna get me in trouble. You gotta think about your career, my boy."

"Yeah, I know what you mean, Charlie. But sometimes, a fellow just gets curious."

"Maybe so. But I always remember what my mama used to say."

"What was that?"

"'Curiosity killed the cat...'"

"Maybe you're right," Hawkins said. "I'll consider the subject closed. Forget the cats, Charlie, let's talk about something else. What do you like to do for fun?"

"Fly planes at breakneck speed."

"Me, too. But I mean in your time off."

"Just standard pilot stuff," Comstock said. "You know: chess tournaments, art museums, the opera, bars, that type of thing. How about you?"

Hawkins grinned. "I like to fish."

Comstock shielded his eyes and glanced around at the scorching desert. He clucked his tongue. "I think you're outta luck, Danny boy. The only thing you're gonna catch around here are scorpions and rattlesnakes."

Hawkins sighed. "I guess you're right. I'm going to request that next time around, I'm stationed right beside a trout stream up in the Rockies somewhere."

Comstock grinned. "Good luck."

As they walked towards the officers' club, a dust devil swirled around, picking up scraps of newspaper and bits of debris. Hawkins watched as it whirled against the sides of the building, then headed out towards the runway.

Just then, a jet passed overhead, cracking the sky in half.

Hawkins smiled. He could hardly wait to get back into the cockpit.

16

CHAPTER FOUR

Hawkins and Comstock spent the next two hours getting to know each other.

Then, at the appointed time, the guard who hadn't left their side looked at his watch and motioned to them.

"A transport is waiting for us outside," he said gruffly.

When they stepped out into the glare of the Sun, they could see a bus waiting with its engine running.

Hawkins noticed that the windows had been blacked out with paint. Once the three of them were aboard and seated, the driver closed a black curtain which hung directly behind his seat, preventing them from seeing ahead.

Hawkins and Comstock exchanged glances. But they didn't ask any questions.

The bus lurched forward. At first, Hawkins thought they might be heading for the hangars he had seen along the runway. But they weren't. They were travelling in a new direction, towards the mountain range on the other side of the dry lake bed.

Twenty minutes later, the bus ground to a halt and the driver opened the curtain.

The guard motioned for them to disembark.

The desert Sun was almost directly overhead. After the darkened bus ride, the glare was almost unbearable. It took several moments for Hawkins's eyes to adjust to the light.

At last, he was able to focus. They were in a valley, surrounded by steep mountains. Nearby, a dry lake bed soaked up the ferocity of the Sun. In many ways, it was a smaller version of the Groom Lake installation. But there were no buildings and no runways.

Then Hawkins noticed a large rectangular hole in the side of the mountain. It seemed to be carved into solid rock.

Shading his eyes with his hand, he suddenly understood. A series of nine hangars, each with its own door, was built directly into the mountainside. The doors slanted down at a sloping angle and were treated with a textured surface paint which blended perfectly with the surrounding landscape. From overhead, the hangars would be virtually undetectable.

Hawkins wondered what kind of aircraft they were testing. After all, there was no runway – just a flat, paved surface adjoining the hangar doors.

One of the hangar doors was completely open. When Hawkins looked inside, he saw Colonel Sheridan talking to a man and a woman in civilian clothes. Moving around them were several security personnel, dressed in camouflage fatigues and carrying automatic rifles.

Then Hawkins saw it – sitting far back in the hangar, almost hidden in shadow.

It was about 12 metres in diameter and maybe 6 metres tall. A ring of lights on the underside of the disk gave off a subdued bluish glow.

At first, Hawkins told himself that this was just some kind of a mock-up, a training device perhaps. But as he got closer, his pilot's instinct told him that this was no fake. Even though his rational mind scrambled for an explanation, in his bones Hawkins knew that what he was seeing was a fully operational flying machine. And he knew that it was not from this world.

"Oh, man," he heard Comstock say, "is *that* what I think it is?"

Hawkins was too stunned to answer.

They walked into the shadow of the hangar, unable to take their eyes from the bluish glow of the craft.

"Welcome to Project Galileo," Sheridan said. His eyes sparkled. He was obviously enjoying the pilots' amazement.

"The purpose of our project is to explore the possibilities of what we call H-PACs, Human-Piloted Alien

Craft. Eventually, we hope to be able to use Earth-based materials to construct operating replicas of the various types of craft in our possession."

Hawkins was astonished.

"You mean you have *more* than one?" he asked.

Sheridan nodded. "We have nine alien craft stored here at S-4. Unfortunately, only three are operational. The others are in various stages of disassembly. We have been back-engineering them, tearing them apart to find out how they work."

"Colonel," Comstock asked, "how did we get these ships?"

"I can give you no further details at this time. One thing you will learn here is that every bit of information you receive will be strictly on a need-to-know basis. The fact that you are curious is natural. I would expect that from any thinking, intelligent person. But your curiosity alone does not constitute a need to know.

"One of the ways we maintain security here is by compartmentalization. No single person knows everything. Each member of the research team understands a piece of the puzzle. When we fit the pieces together, we have an operating system. This way, if there is a weak link in the chain, if someone compromises themselves in some way, it is not a total loss, the damage can be contained within a relatively small area."

"Can we have a closer look?" Hawkins asked.

Sheridan smiled.

"Be my guest," he said nodding to the guards.

The entire disk was supported by a steel scaffolding which rested on huge wheels. Hawkins could see that this enabled the technicians to move the craft back and forth as the need arose.

It was a classic flying saucer shape, with a central hub nearly four metres in diameter, encircled by a gracefully tapered disk. The top of the craft was ringed with what looked like portholes. A small antenna-like projection jutted from the highest point.

Hawkins was astonished to see that there were no rivets, weld marks or joints of any kind. The entire outer skin seemed to be moulded in one complete piece.

"Okay to touch it?" Comstock asked. He had his eye on the guards with the automatic rifles.

"Go ahead," Sheridan said.

Both Hawkins and Comstock walked forward and laid their hands on the edge of the disk, running their fingers over the smooth, slightly lustrous metal. It had a dull, almost aluminum-like finish.

Then they both saw the hatch. It was open. And a metal stairway had been erected to allow access to it.

"Can we go inside?" Hawkins asked.

The Colonel nodded.

He and Comstock climbed the stairway and peered in. They could see that the interior was divided into three levels. Everything was lit with a soft, glowing light which appeared to come from above. The top and bottom levels were not easily visible. But there was plenty to look at in the middle level. Hawkins was surprised to see that there were no steering wheels or joysticks, no consoles or panels or endless switches and gauges, in fact, there was no instrumentation whatsoever.

What was more, there didn't appear to be any wiring or circuitry of any kind. On the floor in the centre of the craft was a discoloured area. It looked to Hawkins as if some type of console had once been there but had since been removed.

It was then that Hawkins saw the chairs and suddenly, the authenticity of the craft struck him like a blow to the head. They were small seats, roughly 30 centimetres high, just big enough for a tiny child to sit in. Chairs built for beings from another world. He placed his hand on the back of the one of the seats, wondering what kind of pilot must have flown this astonishing craft.

As the Colonel appeared in the doorway the interior walls of the craft suddenly began to change. The entire upper half of the craft began glowing, then slowly became transparent, allowing them to look through the metal, as if it were a piece of thick glass. After the walls had been transparent for several minutes, a strange form of writing began to appear on the clear surface.

Hawkins squinted at the figures. They were unlike any alphabetical, scientific or mathematical symbols he had ever seen.

Hawkins stared at the writing for several moments, unable to find words, or even form questions about what he was seeing.

At last, he asked the Colonel: "Do we have any idea what this is all about?"

Colonel Sheridan shook his head and then informed a group of technicians in the lower bay that the demonstration was over.

A moment later, the writing vanished, the transparency began to fade and the inner walls returned to their dull, metallic appearance.

"Well, gentlemen," the Colonel continued, "what do you say we have some lunch with our technical people and talk about how it all works?"

Hawkins turned to face Sheridan.

"Does this thing fly?" he asked.

The Colonel smiled. "Not yet," he said, "but it will. And I want you men to be the ones to put it through its paces."

Comstock grinned at Hawkins.

It was a pilot's dream.

CHAPTER FIVE

The pilots were so overwhelmed by the sight of the craft that they had scarcely noticed the two civilian scientists who had stood patiently in the background watching and waiting.

"Gentlemen," Sheridan said as they walked towards them, "I would like to introduce you to the other half of your research team. This is Dr Herbert Mendelssohn and Dr Barbara Horn."

Hawkins and Comstock shook hands with them. Mendelssohn took off his glasses and began cleaning them with his handkerchief. He was an older, owlish-looking man who spoke with a slight German accent.

"I have always admired pilots," he said. "I think your hands-on knowledge will be a very great asset. I was especially gratified to hear that both of you have a good background in aerodynamic design. Colonel Sheridan is bringing you into this project at a very critical juncture.

"Dr Horn and I have been working for several months on the propulsion system for the craft you see before you. I think we are finally at the point where we are ready to take our ideas from the theoretical to the practical stage."

Dr Horn nodded to a table set up near one wall of the hangar.

"I think it would save time if we talked while we ate," she said. "The cafeteria has sent us some packed lunches. Will you gentlemen join us?"

Hawkins and Comstock nodded dumbly. At that moment, food was the last thing on their minds. The pilots seated themselves at the far end of the table, so they had a clear view of the disk. Colonel Sheridan sat beside them.

Mendelssohn stood before them.

"Our goal in the next hour is to give you a working understanding of the propulsion system which will enable this craft to fly. Your task will be to grasp the concepts we are working on and then help us design flight and navigational controls which will allow you to fly this craft safely and skilfully.

"As I'm sure you noticed, the middle section of the disk contains no pilot controls, no gauges or switches, nothing you would find in a conventional cockpit. Whatever controls you need will have to be built from scratch.

"We will first construct a simulator here in the hangar. When we have that system working properly, we will build an exact replica in the spacecraft. Then, gentlemen, we will wheel the saucer out on to the pad and try our wings.

"Now, I would like to turn the briefing over to Dr Horn. She will give you a solid understanding of the concept behind the propulsion system. Then we will get on to the details of space-time distortion, flying to other galaxies, and so on... Dr Horn?"

The scientist stepped forward. She was tall, at least 30 centimetres taller than Mendelssohn and had sandy coloured, close-cropped hair. Like her colleague, she was dressed simply in casual civilian clothes and sensible shoes.

Dr Horn moved quickly, efficiently. She reminded Hawkins of a bird, pecking at seeds on a sidewalk. When she spoke, it was in a series of breathless, rapidly fired bursts, as if her thoughts were moving too fast for her lips to form the words. Her eyes shone like bright stars.

"Gentlemen," she began. "On the other side of the mountain range, at the Groom Lake installation, the world's most advanced and secret aircraft are being developed and tested. These planes can fly at incredible speeds and manoeuvre with astonishing accuracy.

"But the craft which sits before you is far more advanced. When this craft is operational, it will make the planes which are flying out of Groom Lake seem as primitive as the biplane the Wright Brothers flew at Kitty Hawk.

"Our best information tells us that this disk was built by a race of beings whose technology is at least 50,000 years ahead of ours.

"Think about it: 50,000 years ago, our own species was limited to tools of stone and bone and antler. Agriculture, written communication, domestication of animals – none of these had been developed. The steam engine, the printing press and the multiple nuclear warhead were not even possibilities at that point.

"The extraterrestrial biological entities (we just call then EBEs for short) who designed, built and flew this craft come from a planet outside our Solar System, from the star system known as Zeta Reticuli. They are 37 light years away. You can see these stars from Earth. They are located just below the constellation known as the Big Dipper. But they cannot be seen from the northern latitudes because they are below our horizon.

"The two stars which comprise Zeta Reticuli are almost identical to our Sun. But they are much older. They are the only known examples of two solar-type stars linked together in a binary star system of wide separation. Zeta 1 is separated from Zeta 2 by about a hundred times the distance from our Sun to Pluto.

"The planets which orbit these stars are very similar to ones in our own Solar System. At least one of these planets is much like our Earth. It is the fourth planet out from Zeta 2. We call it Reticulum 4. It contains life much like our own, life that can think and create and has the capability to travel to distant corners of the Universe."

Hawkins had not even taken a bite of his sandwich. He simply held it in his hands, listening.

"Excuse me, Dr Horn," he said. "But before we go on, I have got to ask: How do we know all this?"

The scientist glanced at Colonel Sheridan.

"I am sorry, Major," the officer said, "but that information is beyond your need-to-know. I will say this, however, simply to satisfy your initial curiosity. These craft were given to us by the EBEs as part of a peaceful diplomatic exchange between the United States and the alien visitors."

"They were here?" Hawkins asked.

"Yes, Major," Sheridan said. "They have been observing our planet for at least 25,000 years and have had on-going diplomatic contact with the United States for almost forty years."

As the enormity of the Colonel's comment sank in, Hawkins began to form even wilder questions.

"Are they here now?' he asked.

"No, Major, they are gone."

"And they didn't leave behind an instruction manual?" Comstock joked.

Everyone laughed.

"But, Colonel –" Hawkins began.

Sheridan put up his hand.

"Gentlemen," he said firmly, "I am not authorized to give you any further information about the origins of this craft. I have directed Dr Mendelssohn and Dr Horn to adhere to these rules. What you have just heard is highly sensitive information. I have allowed this data to be passed along to you as a way of satisfying your initial curiosity. But from this moment forward, the present line of inquiry is closed."

Mendelssohn opened a can of soda and poured it into a paper cup.

"This is all very fascinating," he said, "but I think we should get ahead to the practical concerns of our project."

Dr Horn nodded, "I agree completely, Dr. Mendelssohn.

"We must ask ourselves: What kind of technology would enable a ship to travel here from 37 light years away? As you know, a light year is the distance a beam of light would travel in one year's time. According to our present understanding of the laws of the Universe, it is not possible to exceeded the speed of light. The speed of light is 300,000 kilometres per second.

"At that rate, reaching even the closest star system, Proximus Centauri, would take four years. Clearly, the problems of fuel capacity, storage of food and water supplies and a host of other difficulties make a flight of that length impossible, given our present level of technology.

"So, we must ask ourselves: How do they do it? The answer is simple. They do not travel in a linear fashion, from point A to point B. Instead, they use an intense field of gravity to create a space-time distortion which actually bends or folds space, allowing them to travel instantaneously across immense distances.

"Not so long ago, the great scientist and mathematician Albert Einstein theorized that this could be done. But until now, we have never had proof. Einstein speculated that gravity bends time and space. The more intense the gravitational field, the greater the distortion of space and time and the shorter the distances between point A and point B. So that if you could find a way to intensify a very intense gravitational field, you could literally bring the destination to the ship rather than the other way around."

Comstock shook his head.

"Wait a minute," he said, "do you *really* expect us to believe all this? What you're saying sounds like something out of a science fiction movie!"

"It *is* incredible," Dr Horn admitted. "But if you will bear with us, I think we can prove that what we are discussing here is fact, not fiction."

Mendelssohn reached into his briefcase and pulled out a square object.

"I made this crude model as a way of demonstrating what we are saying. I have thumb-tacked a square of rubber to this flat board. Here is a small rock I picked up out in the desert.

"I will place this rock on one end of the rubber sheet. Let's say that this is our spaceship. Suppose our destination is a spot here on the other end of the sheet, which I will mark by drawing a small circle with my pen.

"By focusing your gravity generator on this point you can make space elastic and pull it towards you, just as I am doing now by pinching the rubber and drawing the circle to the rock. When you shut off the gravity generator, space retracts back to its original position. When it does, it takes the stone (or the spacecraft) with it, so the stone is now sitting at its destination. Since time has also been stopped, the journey takes place instantly."

Hawkins nodded.

"I have heard this theory before," he said, "and I have read about it in science fiction books. What I don't understand is how they generate such an intense gravitational pull."

Mendelssohn smiled. "To answer this, gentlemen, we must go inside the ship."

They climbed up the stairway.

"I should not have used the term 'generate' when I talked about the gravitational field because we are not generating anything. All we are doing is accessing and amplifying a gravity wave that already exists.

"Before we plunge ahead, let's return to what we know about gravity itself. One theory is that gravity is a wave and that there are two distinct types of gravity: gravity A and gravity B.

"Gravity A works on a very small scale. We can refer to it as atomic gravity. We see gravity A at work in the nucleus of an atom. Gravity B we could refer to as big gravity. This is the gravity which holds the Earth in orbit around the Sun and holds your feet to the surface of the Earth.

"We know a lot about gravity B. We don't know much about gravity A. Gravity A is very small but very powerful. On the other hand, gravity B is relatively weak; you can momentarily break the force of gravity B by simply jumping in the air.

"So, how do we access and amplify gravity A in order to get a very powerful gravitational field? To do this, we must find an atom that is very heavy – one with a gravity A wave that is so abundant that it extends beyond the perimeter of the atom. Then we can access this gravity field and amplify it, just as we would amplify any other wave. Am I making sense so far?"

Comstock looked sceptical. He furrowed his brow and looked at his partner. But Hawkins did not return his look. He was too busy trying to make sense of the tidal wave of information that was washing over him. The wheel of his mind gripped and spun, like a jeep tyre trying to get traction on a muddy hill. At last, he saw that the others were staring at him, waiting for him to answer.

"Go on," he said quietly.

"Good," Mendelssohn said. "Now, I am sorry to say that there is no naturally occurring element present on Earth heavy enough to contain a gravity A wave this strong. The heaviest element on our periodic chart is uranium, which is 108. This is not nearly heavy enough. What we need is something in the neighborhood of element 115."

Dr Horn opened a box which contained a small disk of orange metal.

"This is element 115," she said. "It is the fuel which powers this craft."

"The ship is powered by an anti-matter reactor," Mendelssohn explained. "This reactor is capable of producing electricity much as our nuclear reactors can. But the fuel, element 115, is not radioactive.

"The electricity produced by this reactor is used to create a gravitational wave which is directed upwards through this central tube, then down along the sides of the craft to the gravity amplifiers. On the underside of the craft are three gravity amplifiers which amplify and focus the gravity wave. They can be arranged into a variety of configurations, depending upon what you wish to accomplish.

"This is the reactor," he said pointing to a metal dome, about the size of half a basketball, which sat in the middle of the floor.

"Not very big," Comstock said.

"It *is* small," Dr Horn commented, "but *very* powerful.

"When a small cone of this element 115 is placed into the reactor and bombarded with protons, it becomes even heavier and becomes element 116. Element 116 decays in a fraction of a second, creating anti-matter.

"When anti-matter combines with matter, we get a tremendous burst of energy, otherwise known as an explosion. The energy generated by one kilogram of anti-matter is equal to the force of forty-seven 10-megaton hydrogen bombs.

"Once this energy is created, we can use a thermoelectric generator to convert it to electricity, which we can use to power the ship. But that is not all. There is still plenty of energy at our disposal. We can use that additional energy to amplify a gravity wave which is so small it barely extends beyond the perimeter of an atom. The gravity wave is directed up this central tube and produces a standing gravitational wave which is so powerful it can distort space and time. About 250 grams of element 115 would probably power this craft for twenty or thirty years, streaking from one end of the Galaxy to another.

"If we are successful in extracting the incredible energy which lies dormant in that small piece of orange rock, this will be an incredible breakthrough. We will have a compact, lightweight, on-board power system which can literally take us anywhere we wish to go."

Comstock shook his head. "That's some fuel," he said. "Does Esso know about this yet?"

Dr Mendelssohn smiled. "What Dr Horn is saying is quite critical. You see, there are more than twenty other scientists here at the facility, working on each of the nine craft, and we are the first team to ever attempt actual flight using 115 as

29

our fuel.

"One of the other teams attempted to use plutonium in their reactor. But the results were disastrous. The pilots crashed on the Nevada test site and were both killed instantly, creating a very hazardous radioactive area out there in the desert."

"What we are learning," Dr Horn said, "is that these craft fly best in a zero-gravity environment. Once they get into an area, like the Earth, which has its own gravity, they need to fly in a different way. We only use one of the gravity amplifiers for this type of flight.

"We direct it towards the ground, sending a gravity A wave downward. As you know, a gravity B wave will naturally be propagating upward from the ground. When we phase shift these two waves together, we can create lift.

"Unfortunately, we suspect that this type of flight is somewhat wobbly. This is why several of the alien pilots have crashed over the years while flying in our atmosphere. I am sure you have all heard the rumours about the 1947 crash in Roswell, New Mexico. We suspect that our own helicopters are much more stable on take-off than these disks."

Colonel Sheridan nodded. "That's why we want to move slowly and do all of our tests in the most conservative manner possible. If you two crash one of these things, we can't just go out to the store and buy another one."

Hawkins looked at Comstock.

"Don't worry, Colonel. We won't crash it, will we, Charlie?"

Comstock smiled, "Heck, no."

"Very well, gentlemen," the Colonel said, "that will be all for today."

Hawkins glanced at his watch.

Talk about space-time distortion. It was already quitting time.

CHAPTER SIX

Despite the unusual nature of the research team's work, their daily schedule soon became routine, almost monotonous. Each morning, Hawkins and Comstock were awakened at 0700 hours. By 0800, after a quick breakfast at the nearly-deserted cafeteria, they would be on the bus, heading to S-4.

Drs Horn and Mendelssohn would arrive by 0900 hours. Colonel Sheridan often dropped by during the day to monitor their progress. And, of course, the Delta Force guards were always there, with their M-16s and their coal-black eyes.

Comstock had heard that the Delta Force troops were a special breed: hard-core military men with no family ties and no compunction about stopping a bullet or pulling a trigger if that was what needed to be done. In any case, he didn't plan to test their resolve.

The research team worked together each day, either in the hangar or in one of the small adjoining rooms. At 1500 hours, the pilots were back on the bus to Groom Lake. In the afternoon, Hawkins and Comstock usually swam in the pool or worked out at the gym or played a fast game of tennis on the clay courts. In the evenings, they drank watered-down beer at the officers' club and told war stories.

Even though their movement around the base was very restricted, the recreational facilities were excellent. The Colonel told them there would be no weekend passes and no leaves, at least for the first few weeks. For the foreseeable future, he told them, Area 51 would be their world.

That was all right with them. Even when they were not on duty they found themselves mulling over the details of the project. Project Galileo required them to draw on all their years of flight experience to create something entirely new, something that had *never* been tried before.

Because the craft had been back-engineered, they had to guess at how the alien pilots actually flew these ships, in much the same way that an archaeologist might make an educated guess about how an ancient people had lived by poring over the artefacts they had left behind.

The thought occurred to Hawkins that this was exactly what they were doing, futuristic archaeology. And he realized, just as every good archaeologist must, that his assumptions could be dead wrong.

The main difficulty they faced was how to construct a set of flight controls that would allow them precisely to control the gravity wave emanating from the reactor.

This was the key to piloting the craft. Without this capability, the disk would never get off the ground. Or, if it did, it would never return in one piece. Hawkins and Comstock were keenly aware of the importance, and the danger, of this dilemma.

There were several major frustrations. For some reason, the original pilot's console had been removed from the craft. No one seemed to know why this had been done or what had become of this essential piece of hardware.

One day, Hawkins suggested that they have a look at the other eight craft in hopes of finding out more about the pilot controls.

"I don't think that will be possible," Dr Mendelssohn said.

Comstock shook his head. "I don't understand. What harm can it do?"

Mendelssohn pursed his lips. "Compartmentalization, gentlemen. You are forgetting our security procedures. Each team is confined to working with their disk alone."

"That's ridiculous," Hawkins protested. "Don't they realize that we could move ahead much faster if we could *share* information? If we all got together, all the scientists and all other the pilots – heck, I don't even know if there are other pilots."

"I can understand your frustration," Mendelssohn said coldly, "but we *must* work within the parameters we have been given. If you have a problem with this, Major, you should speak directly to Colonel Sheridan."

Hawkins just shook his head.

"It doesn't make sense. The right hand doesn't know what the left hand is doing," he said.

Later that day, when Dr Horn and Hawkins were standing apart from the others, the older woman smiled sadly.

"I think that your instincts are right," she confided. "I think that we would progress much more rapidly if there were a free exchange of information. But this is not happening. Because of the security restrictions, we are forced basically to re-invent the wheel.

"I, too, have spoken out against it. But I have been ignored. When I tried to push further, I was told that I would either follow the procedures or I would be dismissed from the project immediately."

At that moment, Mendelssohn appeared from nowhere. Dr Horn dropped her eyes and ended the conversation.

After two weeks, the team was able to piece together a simulator which would allow them to begin testing the pilot's controls. The more complex navigational hardware on the upper bay was clearly beyond their comprehension.

Because there was so much they did not know or understand, they were forced to focus on the basic task of designing controls which would allow them to manoeuvre the craft up and down as well as sideways. They decided that a simple joystick and a few gauges would do for the pilot. The co-pilot would operate the gravity amplifiers. This required an incredible amount of teamwork between the two men. They would switch back and forth, so that each man was equally skilled in both positions.

After nearly a month of painstaking work, they had an

operating set of pilot's controls installed in the disk. The consoles were ugly, almost grotesque, bolted to the floor in the centre of the ship. A maze of electrical wires ran like snakes across the floor of the main compartment. A crew of technicians removed the small chairs and replaced them with low-slung, full-sized pilots' seats. They also had a two-way radio and headsets installed so that the pilots could be in constant communication with Mendelssohn and Horn.

At last, on a scorching morning in mid-August, they were ready for their first test flight. A dozen Delta Force guards ringed the craft as a team of technicians wheeled the disk out on to the pad in front of the hangar.

They used a movable crane to lift the disk from its nesting place on the scaffolding and ferry it outside to the launch.

Colonel Sheridan was on hand, watching everything with sharp, bright eyes. Horn and Mendelssohn stood beside a radio technician who had set up his transmitter under a small canvas awning that had been erected out in the blazing heat of the Sun.

The hatch was opened up and a small metal stairway was placed beneath it.

The first thing Hawkins and Comstock noticed when they entered the craft was the heat.

"Man," Comstock said, "we gotta get an air conditioner in here."

"I would just settle for a desk fan," Hawkins joked.

They had tossed a coin for the pilot and co-pilot position on the first flight. Hawkins lost.

The pilots settled into their seats, fastened their belts and put on their headsets.

The craft was under power now, drawing electricity from the reactor. Comstock and Hawkins sat close together, in their retrofitted chairs. Before them, their makeshift consoles glowed with bright green lights.

Comstock spoke into the microphone that jutted from his headset.

"Base, this is Unit One, do we have commo?"

The radio operator's voice scratched back over their headsets.

"That's an affirmative. Do you hear me?"

"Loud and clear, Base. We are ready for instructions," Comstock said.

Sheridan's voice came in through the radio lines.

"Gentlemen, please be aware that this will be a very short test," he said. "Do not, I repeat, *do not* overextend yourselves or your craft. We are expecting you to proceed with the utmost caution in each and everything you do."

"Roger that, Sir. Caution is the word for the day," Comstock replied.

He turned and winked at Hawkins.

"Very well, men," the Colonel said. "I will now turn you over to Dr Mendelssohn who will coordinate the test from this location."

A moment later, Mendelssohn came on the line.

"This will be just as we practised in the simulator," he announced. "Do we have a check on the electrical systems on your console?"

Hawkins glanced towards his console.

"Check," he said.

Comstock nodded. "Check on the consoles. Everything appears to be working properly."

"Fine," the scientist said. "Let's begin by using your console control to close the hatch."

"Roger that. Closing the hatch now."

Comstock flipped the hatch release and watched as the door slowly lowered into place. It locked down with a slight hiss, leaving them in eerie darkness, with only the glow of the gauge lights to keep them company.

Comstock said, "I am turning on the cabin lights."

"Very well," Mendelssohn replied.

Comstock flicked on an overhead light.

"I've got light," he said.

"That's fine. Now let's bring the transparency effect into play."

Comstock did as he was told. As he flipped the control switch, the metal walls arching around them slowly became transparent. Outside, they could see the hot, arid world of the desert. The puzzling writing began to appear on the glassy inner walls. Hawkins was sure that these squiggles and symbols contained vital information, if only he could decipher them. But there was no time to puzzle over it now.

"Transparency is complete," Comstock said.

"Good," Mendelssohn said. "Now move along to the gravity wave. The amplifiers are running at 100 percent now. Check the position of your generators."

Hawkins checked his gauges.

"They are in the proper configuration," he confirmed.

"All right," Mendelssohn said, "very gently, now, lift a metre or so off the ground."

Comstock turned the amplifier dial up.

"Here we go," he muttered.

There was a slight hissing sound, then, as if by magic, the disk lifted.

Hawkins grinned. They were floating on a gravitational wave, something no earthly pilot had ever done.

Carefully, Comstock guided the craft upwards, keenly aware of how dangerous it would be if the craft fell, even from this modest height.

"Three metres," Mendelssohn reported. "You look good. Continue upwards."

The landscape outside the craft began to look pale and Sun-washed.

"Four metres... five... eight... nine. Stop there. Stop there and simply stand on the wave as steadily as you can."

Hawkins could feel the pulsing of the wave beneath them as they hovered in the air.

"Wonderful! Now let's try the lateral movement we practised," Mendelssohn suggested.

Comstock gripped the joystick and shifted the disk three metres to the right, then to the left.

"Very fine. This is everything we could have asked for," Mendelssohn said. "Now set that thing down."

Gently, Comstock eased up on his control and brought the craft downwards.

All at once, the disk began to wobble and slid to the right.

"What's wrong?" Mendelssohn said urgently.

But Comstock was concentrating too much to engage in idle chatter.

He held the joystick with both hands. For a moment, he thought he was going to crash. But he didn't.

He kept a firm hold on the controls and guided the disk down to a smooth landing, settling on to the pad with just the slightest bit of a wobble.

Comstock turned off the gravity amplifiers. The pilots glanced at each other.

They were both drenched in sweat and grinning from ear to ear.

They turned and silently shook hands.

Comstock flipped the hatch release and the door slowly opened. The desert sunlight came streaming in.

"God bless Sir Isaac Newton," Hawkins whispered.

"And don't forget Dr Albert Einstein," Comstock replied. "I wish those boys were here to see us do this."

Hawkins glanced at the strange writing on the walls around them.

"Who knows?" he said. "Maybe they are."

CHAPTER SEVEN

It wasn't until later that night that Hawkins remembered his wrecked Camaro.

Somehow, in the excitement of his new assignment, he had forgotten about his promise to have the wreckage towed away.

Fortunately, Colonel Sheridan was so pleased with the test flight that he had granted both Hawkins and Comstock a pass for the next weekend. Comstock decided to take the military transport flight down to Las Vegas and try his hand at the blackjack tables. He invited Hawkins to come along.

"No thanks," his partner said. "What we're doing here is enough of a gamble. I don't plan to push my luck."

Comstock wrinkled his brow. "Come on, Danny boy, what are you going to do around here all weekend?"

"I'll entertain myself, don't you worry about that," he said. "Listen, do me a favour, since you're flying down to Vegas, can I borrow your vehicle? I think I'll take a drive out into the desert."

Comstock dug his jeep keys out of his pocket and dropped them into Hawkins's palm.

"Each to his own," he said. "But you're gonna be awful sorry when I fly back here bright and early Monday morning with all of my winnings."

Hawkins grinned. "You'll be lucky if you don't lose your shirt."

Comstock left on Friday night. On Saturday morning, Hawkins climbed into his friend's four-wheel-drive jeep and bumped out across the dusty roads, towards town.

His first stop was at the gas station, where he asked the owner about making arrangements for a tow truck. The mechanic was a red-haired man named Riley who was wearing grease-stained coveralls and smoking a short, foul-smelling cigar.

"Where did you have your accident?" he asked.

"Along 375, out at the Thompson place," Hawkins answered.

"Is *that* so?" Riley, said raising his eyebrows. "Did you run into Mandy?"

"I met the old woman," Hawkins said.

"You're lucky you lived to tell the tale," Riley laughed. "She's all right though, once you get to know her. She's just a little trigger-happy. She winged one of the sheriff's deputies awhile back.

"The poor fellow went out to check on some cattle trouble she was havin' and he no sooner stepped out of his car than she shot him in the shoulder and set her dogs on him. Her eyesight isn't what it used to be, you know. I suppose she thought he was an intruder."

"Mandy's had a hard life. She's all alone out there, except for her boy, Duane. And he hasn't been right for years. He went off the deep end ages ago. I guess he must be in his forties now, but he hasn't been off the ranch in a long, long time."

"So what about the tow truck?" Hawkins asked, anxious to get moving.

Riley sighed and took a drag on his cigar.

"All I can say is I'm not sending a man out there unless you have her expressed permission. I don't want any trouble, you see."

Hawkins nodded.

"Fine," he said. "If I can use your phone, I'll give her a call."

"She hasn't got a phone. She lives pretty far back in the hills and they never got around to running a line out there."

"No problem," the pilot said. "I'll take a drive out there this morning. How do you get to her place?"

Riley wrinkled his brow, thinking about it.

"Go back to where you wrecked the auto," he advised. "Look for a side road heading west off of 375, into the foothills. There used to be a sign for the Circle S Ranch along there somewhere, but it might have blown down. Anyway, it's the only house back in there, you'll find it. Just watch yourself around her dogs. I wouldn't get out of the jeep until she says it's okay."

"Thanks for the advice."

"Fair enough," the mechanic laughed, "and remember, keep your head down. From what I hear, she's still a pretty good shot."

With that comforting advice, Hawkins climbed into the jeep and headed south on Route 375.

He drove for several kilometres before reaching the scene of the accident. As he approached he saw immediately that his Camaro was almost buried in sand. It was as if the earth was now reclaiming it.

Hawkins didn't linger long over the sight. It seemed that the days when he drove the Camaro belonged to another lifetime, a time before he knew the great and puzzling secret which now rested, like a weight, upon his shoulders.

Then, off in the distance, in the shimmering heat, he thought he saw Mandy's pick-up. He put the jeep into four-wheel and rolled off the highway and across the gravel, through sagebrush and gravel piles.

When he got closer, he could see that, sure enough, it was Mandy. She was standing beside her truck, with her hands on her knees, looking down at the ground. At her feet was the bloated body of a dead cow.

She looked up when Hawkins pulled up beside her. But she didn't seem surprised to see him.

Hawkins turned the engine off and stepped out of the jeep, padding across the gravel toward her.

She straightened and nodded down at the cow.

"Now why in God's name would somebody wanta do this?" she asked.

Hawkins looked casually at the cow. It was dead, all right. And covered with flies.

But then he looked again.

Something didn't look quite right. One of the eyeballs was bulging out of its socket and it had turned a milky white. The skin on the lower jaw had been removed, very carefully. The edge of the cut was precise, in a serrated pattern, like a fancy cookie cutter.

"They're at it again," Mandy said.

"Who?" Hawkins asked.

"Whoever's been mutilatin' my cows, that's *who*. This ain't the first time I seen this weird stuff. We had a spate of these back in the '70s. And now, in the last week or so, I've lost four cows this way. Who would wanta do this?" she repeated.

"Possibly predators? Coyotes, maybe?" Hawkins offered.

"Nah. Look at those cuts. I ain't never seen a coyote that can bite in a careful line like this. And look here at the edges of the cut. Looks like it was burned with somethin' mighty hot."

Hawkins looked. He had to admit, it *was* odd.

"Come on over here," Mandy said, motioning for him to follow. "Look at this. Notice how there ain't no cow tracks anywheres along here. The tracks ended about fifty metres over there. It's like it was just picked up by somethin', cut up, then thrown down way over here. But that ain't the weirdest thing about it. What's *real* strange is there ain't any blood."

"What do you mean?"

"No blood on the ground, no blood in the carcass. It's like somethin' just sucked every bit of livin' fluid from this thing and then cast it away, like you'd cast off the empty shell of somethin' you didn't need anymore."

Hawkins just shook his head. Then he had an idea.

"Listen," he said. "I've got a camera in the jeep. Want me to take some pictures? Maybe you could show them to the law enforcement authorities."

Mandy nodded. "Good idea, son. You do that."

Hawkins fetched his camera and took a dozen shots, from several different angles. As he took the pictures, he looked more closely at the wounds. He had to admit it was strange, very strange.

"What are you doin' here?" she asked, as if she were seeing him for the first time.

"I came out to take care of my auto, remember?"

The old woman just shook her head sadly. "I'm not worried about your motor. You can leave it there, for all I care. I'll tell ya, this has me upset. I can understand losin' a cow every now and then. But four in one week – I can't keep up like this. I gotta do somethin' or me and my boy are gonna starve out here."

"I wish I could do something to help," Hawkins said.

Then Mandy cocked her head.

"You do, eh? Well, maybe you can. Listen, you look like you could use a little shade. We ain't much for entertainin' visitors. But if you wanta come over to the place and set with us for a while, you can."

Hawkins nodded. "That'd be good."

Mandy walked to her truck and climbed in. The engine roared to life.

"Just follow me," she yelled.

"I'll be right behind you," the pilot said.

Mandy turned the truck around and headed for the foothills.

Chapter Eight

It was a torturous drive back to the ranch, even with four-wheel drive. Hawkins could not comprehend how Mandy's antique truck could make it. But somehow, she negotiated the harsh terrain with an ease and grace that amazed him. They followed a network of dry watercourses and rutted roads until they pulled up on to a gravel road that wound up into the foothills.

They had been driving for a good twenty minutes before Hawkins saw a ramshackle ranch house set in a dusty hollow beside a dry spring.

As soon as they came within sight of the house, a dozen snarling dogs burst from their hiding places underneath the porch. They circled the jeep looking so fierce that Hawkins regretted that he hadn't thought to put the top up.

"Nice place," Hawkins shouted as he pulled to a stop in the front yard.

"The heck it is," Mandy shouted. Then she whistled shrilly to her dogs.

"Git back from there!" she hollered. "The whole bunch of ya! Git to the porch!"

The dogs cowered and scampered back to their shadowy place of rest underneath the wooden porch. Hawkins could see that the porch timbers were old and sagging. Here and there, some of the floorboards were missing. It was a cinderblock construction with a rusted sheet metal roof. The stump of a blackened stove pipe poked up through the sheet metal.

The porch itself was cluttered with piles of junk – dead and rusting machinery, a dilapidated couch and heaps of old farm tools. Everything was either broken or used up.

Out back, Hawkins could see a jumble of wooden sheds

and out buildings. They were in poor repair, so flimsy that Hawkins thought a strong wind might blow them over.

With an eye on the dogs, Hawkins slipped out of his vehicle and walked to the porch. On the other side of the tattered screen door, he saw a man about his age, wearing a wrinkled set of blue pyjamas. He was bald and pot-bellied and had thick glasses. He looked as if he had tried to shave that morning, got half-way through the job, then given up out of sheer boredom.

"Flyboy," Mandy said as she swung the door open, "this here is my youngest, Duane."

The man extended a shaking hand. Hawkins took it. He felt as if he were holding a dead fish.

"I'm Danny Hawkins," the pilot said.

"Good tameetcha," Duane said shyly.

Hawkins nodded. He stepped into the doorway.

The inside of the ranch house was similar to the outside. Everything was in a shambles. It was basically one large room, a kitchen and living room all in one. Two bedroom doors opened off a small hallway in the back. Hawkins didn't dare ask where the bathroom was.

The old woman looked around the room as if she had misplaced something.

"Listen, Hawkins," she said, "are you a drinkin' man? We don't have any electricity, so we don't have anythin' cold. But I do got some peppermint schnapps around here somewhere."

"That's all right, Mrs Thompson –"

"Call me Mandy."

"All right, Mandy. Listen, it's a little early in the day for schnapps. I'd settle for just a cool glass of water and a bite of something to eat."

The old woman turned to Duane.

"Go fetch us a jug of that well water. And bring us some of them crackers, will ya, Honey?"

Duane nodded and disappeared into the kitchen.

All three went out on to the front porch and sat in the slight shade, eating dry biscuits out of a cardboard box and drinking rusty-tasting well water out of plastic cups.

"Another cow's gone, Duane," Mandy announced.

"Another one?' he said dumbly.

"Yeah. Hawkins here got some pictures of it. It's the darndest thing."

"I saw the searchlights," Duane said.

"I know you did, Honey."

"Danny," he said, "I saw the lights, at night, down there by the spring."

Hawkins took a deep breath and decided to enter the conversation.

"You saw them last night?" he asked.

"No," Duane said. "Not this time. I didn't see anythin' this time. But last time – when was it, Ma?"

"Back in the '70s Honey, years ago."

"Yeah, back in the '70s, years ago... I saw the lights on our cows. I think it was helicopters. They came and carried the cows off and cut them up."

"Who do you think did it?" Hawkins asked.

"Government," Mandy said bitterly. "Your people. They're cartin' off my cows and cuttin' them up, drainin' out their blood."

"But why?" Hawkins asked.

Mandy turned to face him. He could tell she was starting to get worked up about it.

"I was hopin' you might know," she said. "Oh, I ain't askin' you to reveal none of your top-secret business. I ain't askin' for that. All I'm sayin' is this: if you know somethin' I can do to keep them helicopters from gettin' my cows, I sure wish you'd just go ahead and tell me."

Hawkins shook his head. "I don't know anything about it."

"All right, then," Mandy said, rocking in her chair, "if that's how you're gonna be."

Hawkins could have got up then and just walked to the

45

jeep and driven away. But he didn't. For some reason, he wanted to sit on the porch with these two hermit-like people, and eat crackers and drink well water.

At noon, when the angle the of Sun made everything look pale and lifeless, they went inside the house. Mandy opened a jar of pickles and they sat around the kitchen table, eating the long, slippery slices with their fingers.

"I still got that headache," Duane said during one of their long, digestible silences. The sunlight coming in through the windows reflected off his glasses.

Mandy nodded. "Did you try that willow twig tea?"

He nodded.

"Did it help?"

"A little," Duane said. He turned to Hawkins.

"Have you ever had a real bad headache?" he asked. "One that feels like somebody dropped a cinderblock right on your forehead?"

Hawkins shook his head. "I've never had one *that* bad," he admitted.

"Well," Duane said wearily. "I get 'em all the time. Sometimes it gets so bad I just gotta go in my room and draw the curtains and lay down in the dark until it's over."

"It ain't natural," Mandy put in. "He didn't have 'em as a kid. Heck, if you wanta know the truth, I think it had somethin' to do with them Government tests. I bet them helicopters that are takin' the cows are sprayin' something out here on my land, some kinda chemical. I bet that's what's givin' him these headaches."

Duane rubbed his forehead with a shaking hand.

"I'd say these headaches and the cattle thing started about the same time, don't you think so, Mama?"

Mandy nodded.

"No question about it," she said. "Up until then, Duane was a good worker. He used to help me on the place. But he ain't been able to go outside and work for years. All he can do is sit in the house and make them funny pictures."

"Pictures?" Hawkins asked.

"Duane's a bit of an artist," Mandy explained. "Say, Duane, go ahead and show him somethin' you've drawed up."

"Aw, Mama..."

"Now, go on. Bring out that drawin' pad. I want Mr Hawkins to see the kinda thing my boy can do."

Reluctantly, Duane rose and went back into a side room. He returned a moment later with an over-sized drawing block under his arm. His mother moved the jar of pickles and Duane laid the pad down on the table. Then he flipped open the cover, revealing the first drawing.

Hawkins couldn't believe his eyes.

"He has quite an imagination," Mandy said when she saw Hawkins's expression.

Hawkins tried to form words, to ask questions, but he could not.

Duane didn't seem to notice his astonishment. He began flipping through page after page of coloured pencil illustrations, each one more realistic than the last.

It was all there. The shape, the scale, the lights around the edge, the archways. Even the details of the hatch were precise and clear. It wasn't quite an exact replica of the ship they had been working on, but it was awfully close.

At last, Hawkins's ability to speak returned. "Where did you get all this?"

"Well," Duane said modestly, "like Mama says, I've got a pretty good imagination..."

"He is a real drawer," Mandy put in, "don't you think so?"

Hawkins nodded as Duane flipped through his collection. At last, they came to a black and white pencil sketch of the interior of the craft, a cut-away view that showed three small chairs and three consoles. The dome of the reactor and the long tube of the wave guide were clearly visible.

"Oh, Lord," Hawkins thought, "he's been *inside* one of these things."

As soon as the thought occurred to him, he pushed it

away. But, as the moments flowed by, his grappling mind couldn't come up with any other explanation.

"Duane," Hawkins said at last, "your mother is right. You are a very fine artist. Would you allow me to take these drawings back and show them to some of my friends?"

"Do you think somebody would buy them?" Duane asked.

"I'm sure they would," Hawkins answered.

"We could sure use the money," Mandy put in, surprised by this sudden turn of fortune.

Duane beamed.

"I've got some other ones in the back, too. But they're of horses. That's what I like to draw, mostly: horses and spaceships."

Hawkins just nodded. He sat through another hour of Duane's equestrian drawings. Then he stood up.

"I have to go," he announced.

"All right," Mandy said, drying the pickle juice off of her hands with a towel.

"When you gonna let us know about them drawin's?"

"I'll be out next weekend, I promise."

Hawkins rose and placed the pad of disk drawings under his arm.

"Hey, Danny," Duane said, "you forgot the horse ones. Don't you want them too?"

"Oh, sure," Hawkins said, "of course I do. Give 'em to me, will ya?"

Duane stacked up the sketchbooks and loaded them under Hawkins's arm.

In a few moments, he was past the dogs, into the jeep and driving away with the sketchbooks safely stowed on the seat beside him.

Hawkins could scarcely believe it. Once he was out of sight of the ranch house, he stopped the jeep and sat there in the blazing Sun, poring over each drawing, absorbing the details, and muttering, "How?"

Hawkins didn't have an answer. But he intended to find one.

Chapter Nine

Hawkins spent the rest of the weekend mulling over his next move.

He considered showing the drawings to the rest of the research team first thing on Monday morning, even calling Colonel Sheridan in on the case. But something told him that this would have to be handled more discreetly.

The way he saw it, Sheridan and Mendelssohn might get worried about security issues and confiscate the drawings. If that happened, he might never see the illustrations again. That would be an incredible loss.

Hawkins thought next of Comstock. By all rights, he knew he should be able to trust his partner. But, as he thought about it more clearly, he wondered if it might be better to leave Charlie out of the loop. For all of his easy-going ways, Comstock was a pilot who went strictly by the book. He did what he was told, no more and no less.

What would happen if Comstock insisted on obeying the chain of command and taking this startling piece of information directly to the Project Director? Hawkins knew he couldn't take that chance.

That left Dr Horn. Hawkins thought about it for a long time. She seemed dissatisfied with the way the project was being conducted and might welcome some input from an outside source. On the other hand, she just might turn him in for trying to circumvent the security procedures. But, somehow, he doubted it. Something told him that he should place his trust in Barbara Horn.

He kept the drawings hidden under his mattress. They would stay there, he decided, until he was ready to bring them out. Then he would share what he knew and let the chips fall where they may.

On Monday morning, Comstock arrived on the early morning flight, along with Mendelssohn and Horn.

They all rode the bus together out to S-4.

"How did it go in the big city?" Hawkins joked.

Comstock grinned. "I won big, man."

"Really? How much did you win?"

"I peaked at $10,000."

"What do you mean you peaked?"

"I mean that was the highest amount I won."

"Fine. So just give me the final figure. How much did you come home with?"

Comstock was silent.

"Charlie, you're not saying anything."

"I'm thinkin', man. I'm thinkin'."

"Okay."

"I'd say I have about fifteen cents left."

"But you said you won big."

"I did, I did. But then I lost big. But that's the way it goes. By the way, how did you make out? You didn't wreck my jeep, did you?"

"Your jeep is safe and sound," Hawkins reported. "And I have to tell you, it was pretty boring without you around."

"Really?"

"Oh, yeah."

"Well," Comstock said, "maybe you'll appreciate me more, now that I'm back."

"Sure will," Hawkins smiled.

That morning the team laid out their flight schedule for the next month. They decided to fly once a week, on Wednesday nights. This way there would be less chance of them being spotted by curious onlookers. The plan was to make very careful tests of the flight capabilities of the craft without actually leaving the Earth's atmosphere. That was quite ambitious, everyone agreed.

Later, at lunch, Hawkins had a chance to talk privately with Dr Horn. With a wary eye on the others, he explained what he had discovered and why he felt that it should be handled with the utmost discretion.

She did not disappoint him. She did not treat him as if he was crazy. And she did not rush off to tell the others.

"This is exciting news," Dr Horn said, "even if it is a *little* unconventional."

"I don't know how much this guy knows," Hawkins told her, "and I don't know how he knows it. Look, I'll admit it sounds crazy. But I can't think of any other explanation. I'm sure you will agree once you see the drawings. I swear he's been inside an alien craft. But he has no conscious memory of it. How is that possible?"

Dr Horn shook her head.

"I don't know," she said quietly.

"If we can somehow access the information in his muddled brain," Hawkins said, "we might be able to get some critical clues about how these craft are actually flown. It could save us months of work. Remember what you said about trying to find a way to avoid reinventing the wheel? This is it!"

Horn nodded.

"What you are saying is very hard to believe, Major Hawkins. But then, this entire project has been filled with amazing revelations. Tell me, does this fellow – what is his name again?"

"Duane Thompson."

"Yes. Does Duane claim to have seen UFOs out on their land?"

"Not at all. He says he thought he saw helicopters picking up their cows. Oh, and there is something else: he has had chronic and debilitating headaches for years now. He and his mother think his physical troubles are linked to Government chemical experiments out on their land."

Dr Horn frowned thoughtfully.

"This is definitely outside of my area of expertise," she admitted. "But I do have a colleague in Los Angeles who might be able to help us. His name is Benjamin Talbot. Dr Talbot is a psychiatrist who specializes in treating people who have undergone traumatic experiences. Many of his patients are veterans of wars or victims of violent crimes.

"He once told me that psychological trauma is often accompanied by some type of physical manifestation – chronic headaches are among the most common. He has been very successful in using hypnotic regression as a way of accessing unconscious memories. He uses hypnosis to help trauma victims re-explore and work through their traumatic experience, improving both their physical and psychological health.

"I suppose it is possible that Duane is suffering from some type of trauma. Or he is suffering from hallucinations."

"Well, Dr Horn," Hawkins persisted, "I'd like someone to explain the cattle mutilations and the accuracy of the drawings."

"Do you think Duane would agree to being hypnotized?" Horn asked.

Hawkins kept his voice low.

"I don't know. But I'll try to find out."

"I would like to see those drawings," Horn said.

"Yes. I will smuggle them out here tomorrow and you can have a look at them yourself."

Their conversation was brought to a close when Mendelssohn beckoned to them. He and Comstock had been going over some paperwork at a lab table on the other side of the room.

"I'll try to connect with Dr Talbot this week," Horn whispered. "And Hawkins – I want to thank you for placing your trust in me. I think you will have to be very careful about revealing what you know. As I have mentioned before, I do not always think that the people who administer this program understand the true nature of scientific research. I find some of their restrictions endlessly frustrating. Be careful. Your desire to known the truth *could* be misunderstood."

Hawkins nodded. Then they went back to work.

The pilot felt as if he had crossed a dangerous line. If Dr. Horn could be trusted, she would be an important ally. If she turned against him, Hawkins would be in deep trouble. He thought momentarily about the secrecy contract he had signed. Hawkins had to admit that he was afraid. But his years of flying had taught him that the best way to combat fear is to face it head-on. That way, it either consumes you or disappears entirely.

The next day, Hawkins flew directly into the face of his fears. He passed the drawings to Dr Horn in a plain brown envelope. She took them with her that night, had them photocopied, and returned the originals.

"What did you think?" he asked after she had seen the sketches.

"Very compelling," Dr Horn agreed. "But the illustrations did not show us anything we don't already know. What we really need to establish is how the pilot actually controlled the craft."

Hawkins nodded.

Just then, Mendelssohn stepped forward with a quizzical look on his face.

"Is everything okay?" he asked in an unusually gruff voice.

"Yes. Although I was just saying that I wished we had more information about how the pilots flew the crafts," Dr Horn replied, her face flushing red.

"Indeed," Mendelssohn said. "You two seemed to be concerned about *something*."

"That's right, Sir," Hawkins said, stepping into the breach. "I was just saying that I would like to make some scale drawings of the interior of the craft to use in our planning."

Mendelssohn's eyes were cold and hard. "I see," he said at last.

Hawkins's heart was pounding. As they walked over to the

worktable, he felt a trickle of sweat running down his back. He wondered how much of their conversation the good doctor had *actually* heard.

The second test flight took place, as scheduled, on Wednesday evening. It was a clear night with no wind, perfect flying conditions.

This time, Hawkins was in the pilot's seat. Comstock had coached him on the best way to ride the controls to prevent wobble. ·

In the beginning, Hawkins was instructed to see how much manoeuvrability they could achieve, riding less than a metre above the ground. Then they would test the response of the craft at greater heights.

Even though it was a cool night, Hawkins was already sweating when he climbed into the pilot's seat. But he really didn't need to worry. Things went remarkably well.

The design of the controls allowed him to make minute changes in the intensity of the gravity A wave emanating from the bottom of the craft. Hawkins played with this for almost an hour before he felt confident that he was in complete control. With the transparency effect at work, he had a clear 360-degree view of the darkened landscape around him.

"I'd like to take it up for a more extensive flight test," he told Mendelssohn.

The scientist's voice crackled over the headset.

"Are you confident?" he asked.

"Yes," Hawkins said. "I have the low altitude manoeuvrability pretty well under control. We talked before about how the intensity of the wave might change as the craft gains altitude. Shall we proceed with a graduated altitude test?"

"Very well," Mendelssohn said. "Proceed as discussed."

Hawkins glanced over at his partner.

"Got your seat belt fastened, Charlie?"

Comstock nodded.

"Go for it, buddy."

Hawkins gently turned the amplifier knob, increasing the intensity of the wave beneath them. With a soundless grace, the craft began scaling upwards. At ten metres, Mendelssohn reported that the surface of the ship was glowing with an intense blue light. At fifteen metres it changed to what he described as a sodium yellow. At thirty metres the scientist informed them that the craft was glowing with a fiery orange colour.

"It's magnificent!" Mendelssohn said.

"What's happening?" Hawkins asked. "Why are we changing colour?"

"The fluorescent tubes that light the ship are interacting with the atmosphere. Of course, in space there is no atmosphere to interact with – so you would not get this type of display. However, here on Earth, the atoms in the fluorescent tube are interacting with the nitrogen in the air. That's what gives you the whitish blue – the same colour as lightning."

"Understood. So at different power levels you're going to get different colours?"

"Exactly."

"Shall we bring her down now?" Hawkins asked.

"Yes. By all means. Let's not push our luck."

Hawkins gently brought the craft down to a soft landing on the pad.

"How did you like it?" Comstock asked as soon as the hatch was open.

Hawkins smiled in the darkness of the disk.

"What's not to like? It floats like a dream."

Comstock laid a hand on his partner's shoulder.

"Welcome to the Earth's most exclusive pilot's club," Comstock said.

That night, back at their quarters, Comstock glanced around Hawkins's room.

"You sure do like these horse drawings, don't you?" he

commented. He gestured to the sketches thumbtacked up around his room.

"Sure do," Hawkins said.

Actually, he was paying good money for every one of them. He was going to give Duane $50 apiece for each of the sketches, whether they were disks or horses. Considering that it was all coming out of his own pocket, it seemed a stiff price to pay. But if they could learn more about the craft, Hawkins knew that the investment would be worth it.

On Friday afternoon, Dr Horn drew Hawkins aside.

"I talked with Dr Talbot," she said quietly. "As a favour to me, he has agreed to fly out next weekend and conduct a hypnotic regression, free of charge. But he wants you to lay the groundwork. He cannot go ahead without the permission of both the subject and his mother."

Hawkins nodded.

"How would we set it up?"

"Myself, Dr Talbot and you would have to meet at the Thompson place. The ranch is an ideal location, remote and quiet, far from the inquiring eyes of our friends in security. There, Dr Talbot would conduct a tape-recorded hypnotic regression with Duane. Of course, his mother would be present the entire time. Do you think they would agree to something of that nature?"

"They might, if I phrase it in the right way," Hawkins said. "Listen, I've been thinking. I want the technical information just as much as you do. But I don't want to do anything that's going to harm Duane."

"I understand. I asked Dr Talbot about that. He told me that, while he can't make any guarantees, his experience has been that these regressions usually move the patient in a positive direction, both physically and mentally. I think it's worth a try."

Hawkins nodded.

"I'll let you know," he said. "I plan to see them this weekend."

"Oh, Major Hawkins..."

"Yes?"

"Be careful. I think both you and I know how dangerous this could become if our plans find their way into the wrong hands."

Hawkins nodded grimly. He thought again about the confidentiality agreement he had signed. And the punishments that might lie ahead. Then he swept those thoughts away. More than *anything*, he wanted to know how to fly that craft.

On Friday afternoon, Comstock began making his preparations for a trek to the big city.

"Can I use your jeep, again?" Hawkins asked.

"You can use it all you want," Comstock said. "What I don't understand is why you're so fascinated by this dried-up, God-forsaken corner of the Universe."

"The desert is a beautiful place, Charlie," Hawkins replied.

On Saturday morning, Hawkins drove out to the ranch. When he pulled up in a trail of dust, the dogs came bounding from underneath the porch, leaping around his car. But Hawkins was not intimidated by them any more.

"Get back, you mangy hounds," he shouted playfully.

Duane appeared at the door. He was as scruffy-looking as ever.

"Hello there, Danny!" he called out. "I got some more drawin's for you."

"That's good," Hawkins said. "Where's your Ma?"

"Out back, hangin' clothes. Wanta see my new sketches?"

"In a moment, Duane. First off, I want to talk with your Ma for a few minutes," he said.

Hawkins walked around to the back and there was Mandy, hanging a row of overalls on a dirty clothesline strung between the house and one of the gravity-defying sheds.

"Hello, Mandy," he called.

The old woman looked up.

"Well," she said. "Look what the wind blew in. I'll be done here in a minute. I got a fresh jar of pickles and Duane's got some artwork to show you."

"I've got good news," Hawkins said. "I sold every one of his drawings. Got a good price for them, too: fifty dollars each."

Mandy smiled.

"I swear," she said, "it'll do that boy a heap of good to know that. And with the cattle business what it is, the money'll come in real handy."

"Listen, Mandy," Hawkins said. "There's something else I gotta talk to you about."

She turned from the flapping clothes.

"What is it? You don't think you can sell any more of the drawin's?"

"No, it's not that. In fact, Duane's artwork has attracted the interest of some people I know. They think that Duane could be a really good artist. I told them about his problem with the headaches and how it keeps him from working. Listen, I found a doctor who thinks that there may be some link between Duane's headaches and the incident with the helicopters –"

"Well, of course there's a link," Mandy said impatiently, "that's what we've been tellin' ya all along. It's the Government that's done this to him –"

"Mandy, don't get all worked up about it. Just listen to me for a moment. The doctor thinks that Duane may have been so frightened by the whole thing that it's put his system out of balance and is causing him to have these terrible headaches. You see, his memory of what happened that night could be so deeply buried that even he isn't aware of what *really* happened. Sometimes the mind works like that, sort of as a way of protecting itself."

Mandy shook her head sadly. "Sounds pretty complicated to me. All I know is I'd give most anythin' if I could find a way to put that boy right again."

Hawkins took a breath and plunged ahead.

"This doctor is a psychologist who uses hypnosis to help people work through their memories and sort them out. He says he'd be willing to come out here next weekend and conduct a hypnotic session with Duane to see if he can uncover the source of the memories."

Mandy frowned.

"Hypnosis, huh? Sounds kinda radical to me."

"I don't think so. It is a practice used by many well-regarded psychiatrists and psychologists."

"This fella, what's his name?"

"Dr Talbot."

"He from around here?"

"No, he's from Los Angeles."

"What's he chargin'?"

"He's not charging anything. He's doing it as a favour to me."

"And he's a real doctor?"

"Yes, he's a medical doctor."

"Well," Mandy said, "it's not the kinda thing I would have thought of doin'. But if Duane is willin', I'll go along."

"Good. Now all we need to do is convince him."

'I don't think that'll be hard. In case you ain't noticed, that boy practically worships the ground you walk on."

Hawkins nodded. He hoped he was not betraying the trust that had been placed in him. He hoped that what they were about to do would benefit everyone, Duane included.

"Come in the house," Mandy said, "them pickles are waitin'."

CHAPTER TEN

The dogs wouldn't stop barking the day Dr Horn, Dr Talbot and Major Hawkins converged on the ranch. Each one drove in from a different direction. It was the most activity the Thompson ranch had seen in years.

The dogs were edgy. Mandy and Duane were clearly nervous as they went through awkward introductions.

Dr Talbot was a big, barrel-chested man with close-cropped white hair and a white goatee. When they were seated around the kitchen table, he began to speak.

"Mrs Thompson, I want to thank you for inviting me into your home. And Duane, I want to thank you for your willingness to undergo what may prove to be a very difficult experience.

"My colleague, Dr Horn, believes that the illustrations you have made could only have been drawn by someone who has actually been inside a spaceship. What do you think of that idea, Duane?"

Duane laughed nervously.

"I think that sounds crazy," he said.

"Yes, it does sound a little crazy doesn't it? When Dr Horn called me, I found it hard to believe myself. But I know Dr Horn very well. She would not have called me unless she felt she had something worth investigating. So I've decided to see what we can find out.

"Until the past few days, I knew very little about UFO sightings and even less about the psychological effects they might have on people. Like most people, I thought that people who report seeing UFOs must be either lying or crazy. But in the last week I have taken it upon myself to look into the professional literature and to talk to a few of the specialists in the field.

"What I have learned is that there is a small but growing number of well-respected psychiatric professionals who believe that *some* of the people who are reporting these sightings are not crazy or delusional. In fact Duane, you, and a lot of other people, could be suffering from something called post traumatic stress syndrome. This is the same malady that effects survivors of airline crashes and veterans of wars. It occurs when an event takes place which disrupts an individual's daily routine. This event can be so powerful that it derails their usual methods of coping."

He looked at Duane.

"Am I making sense, son?"

"Kind of," Duane replied. "But I never said I saw any flyin' saucers. I think what I saw were helicopters."

"I know that, Duane. This leads me directly into my next thought. You see, when the mind experiences something which is so traumatic that it has the potential to shatter the psyche of the viewer, a strange survival mechanism kicks into play.

"As a way of coping, the mind will sometimes create what we call a screen memory. It will replace the memory of the upsetting event with something more palatable, almost as if a screen had been drawn and something less disruptive had been projected on to the screen. Do you see what I'm getting at?"

Mandy frowned.

"So, let me get this straight," she said. "Are you sayin' that my boy might have really seen a UFO pickin' up our cows but that all he remembers is this here screen memory of helicopters?"

"Yes, Mrs Thompson, that is exactly what I am saying. But, understand, this is only a theory. To find out the truth, we would actually have to go back into Duane's memory and see what we can find.

"I am a certified psychiatrist in the State of California and have been doing hypnotic regressions with my patients for over twenty years. I have found this to be an excellent way of recovering previously buried memories."

He leaned forward.

"Duane, what I want to do is to put you in a light hypnotic trance and return you to your memory of the night you saw the cow drawn up into the sky. I'll have you lying on the couch over there. I'll have a tape recorder running and you will narrate your memories to us as they occur. Afterwards, I will give you a copy of the tape to listen to as much as you like.

"Hopefully, this procedure will alleviate some of the stress you have felt. I understand that you have been suffering from chronic and severe headaches. Do I understand correctly that these headaches began only after the incident with the helicopters?"

Duane nodded.

"All right. Well, if we do nothing else today, I hope that we can at least improve the incidence of these debilitating headaches. Do I have your permission to proceed?"

Duane looked nervously at his mother.

"Mama?"

"It's for you to say, Honey," his mother said.

Duane swallowed.

"All right," he said. "I'll do it."

The dogs were quiet now.

Duane lay on the couch with his sneakers off, staring at the ceiling.

"Let's begin with a few relaxation exercises," Dr Talbot suggested.

Duane closed his eyes and followed the path laid out by the psychiatrist's slow, comforting voice. Within a few moments, his facial muscles began to sag. His lips parted slightly. The tension seemed to drain from his limbs and his body lay like a lump of clay on the couch.

The room was very quiet except for a slight hum coming from Talbot's battery-operated tape recorder. Everyone sat on their kitchen chairs, as still as statues.

"Can you hear me, Duane?" Talbot asked.

Duane's voice was foggy and dreamlike, as if he were just waking from a long sleep.

"Yes," he said quietly.

"Fine. Now, the purpose of this session will be to return you to the events of June of 1979, when you spotted one of your cows being lifted into the air. Let yourself drift back now, from the present day to that evening in 1979. You will be able to go back in time. You will be able to see and hear and feel just as you did back then. You will be able to talk and describe your impressions as they occur to you. All right, go ahead, describe what you see."

"I am on the porch," Duane said.

"Of this house?"

"Yeah."

"Is there anyone with you?"

"No. Mama is asleep in the house."

"I understand. Now, describe what you see."

"It's dark. A lot of stars. Late at night. The dogs are barkin'. I get up and came out on to the porch to see what is happenin'."

"Good. And what do you see?"

"A light. It's like a searchlight, comin' down from somethin' up in the sky. At first I think it must be a helicopter because it's kinda hovering there. But then I realize that if it was a helicopter I would hear the – what do you call them?"

"The rotor blades?"

"Yeah. The things that whirl around. But I can't hear anythin'."

"Can you see the object that the light is coming from?"

"No, I can't see anythin' up there. All I see is the light. But it doesn't look like a normal beam of light. It's more solid than that. It almost looks like when a shaft of light comes in the window and has pieces of dust dancin' around in it."

"Okay, you're doing fine. What's happening now?"

"The spotlight is on one of our cows, down there by the spring. And now – here's the strange part – the cow is bein' lifted up into the light."

"How? Do you see any ropes or cables?"

"No. Nothin' like that. I can see it squirmin', tryin' to get free. It's almost like it's just bein' sucked up by the beam of light."

"Okay. What's happening now?"

"I am steppin' off the porch, walkin' towards the light. I am tryin' to figure out what's goin' on. I am lookin' up but I can't see anythin', it's too dark. All I see is the dark sky..."

"Okay, Duane. You are doing really well. Now let's see if we can go even deeper. I want you to descend farther into this memory, as if you are walking down two more flights of stairs, down into a deep, deep well. Allow yourself to do that."

"I am there."

"Good. What do you see?"

"I am on the porch."

"Good."

"I am steppin' off the porch now. I'm walkin' over to the spring. The dogs aren't comin' with me, they are hangin' back for some reason."

"Are they still barking?"

"Yeah, they're barkin' – now, wait – the light is on me! I'm in the light! I'm in the light now! It's a bright light. Real, real bright. Doctor, can I stop now? I want to stop. I'm real scared."

"Stay with it, Duane. Tell us what you see."

"No, I *really* don't want to. I want to come back. I'm afraid..."

"Duane, listen to me. Your fear is real, but it can't hurt you. Push on through."

Duane's body began to tremble violently, as if he were shuddering from cold.

"Duane?"

"Yes?" His voice was shaky, full of emotion. Tears began to slide down his cheeks.

"What's happening now?"

"I'm inside."

"Inside what?"

"The space ship."

"How do you know it's a space ship?"

"I just know."

"All right. Describe what you see."

"It's pretty big. Maybe 6 metres across. A big dome with a lot of lights. In the centre is a table. The cow is on the table, being cut up."

"You see the cow being cut up?"

"Yes."

"How is it being cut up?"

"Some kind of light beam. Real thin."

"I see. What else?"

"There are people here. Well, they are not people exactly. They are more like insects. They move around like insects. They kind of pivot like a grasshopper does when it moves."

"Can you describe them?"

"They have big heads, small bodies. There are maybe five or six of them. They are not payin' any attention to me. They are workin' on the cow."

"How tall are they?"

"Maybe a metre tall."

"Eyes?"

"Dark, almond-shaped eyes, like an insect."

"Nose?"

"Real small, just two holes for the nose."

"Mouth?"

"Real small. No lips."

"How about the hands?"

"Sorta delicate, like claws."

"Any clothes?"

"Like a silver jumpsuit. Just the hands and the face showin'."

"Do they talk or make any sound?"

"Yeah. But they don't talk to me. They are just ignorin' me. It's as if they know I'm here, but they are too busy to do anythin' with me yet. They are talkin' to each other. It sounds like when somebody holds your nose. It has a funny, very quick sound to it."

"Fine. Just let yourself be aware of what's happening before you. What are they doing now?"

"They are cuttin' up the cow. They are workin' real quickly, real efficiently. Each one does a certain job. Now they are hookin' up tubes. Stuff is movin' through the tubes and emptyin' into a big basin."

"What kind of stuff?"

"Blood, I guess. Listen, I'm not supposed to know any of this. I wasn't supposed to be seein' this."

"How do you know? Did they tell you you weren't supposed to be seeing this?"

"Yeah."

"Did they speak to you?"

"Not in words, no."

"In some other way?"

"Yes. They can speak to me mind-to-mind. Like a voice in the centre of my head."

"I see. What did they say?"

"They said they were takin' samples. I asked them what for. I start askin' them a lot of questions."

"Okay. Do they respond?"

"When they want to answer me, they do. Otherwise, they just ignore me. They are real busy with the cow."

"Okay. What do they tell you?"

"They say that they have been conductin' these tests for a long time and will go on doin' them. They say somethin' real bad is in the cow's fluids and they have to find out how concentrated it is. They say it started out in the ground and then it went to the water, then into the plants that the cow eats and now it's in the cow. They say that when a person eats the cow, then it goes into them."

"Some kind of poison?"

"Yeah. Some kinda pollution. They say that if it doesn't stop there's gonna be a big loss of life."

"Human life?"

"All kinds of life."

"I see. What is the poison?"

"Some kinda chemical. They are tellin' me, but I don't know what they're talkin' about."

"Okay. Let yourself relax and focus in on what you are being told. What is the chemical?"

"It's...Pluto, somethin'..."

"The planet Pluto?"

"No. Plutonium. That's it. That's the stuff that's gonna kill everythin', they say. Unless we do somethin' about it. They say it's gonna start a kinda chain reaction. I ask them if they are tryin' to help us but they don't answer. It seems like they are just watchin' us and collectin' samples but not helpin' us to do anythin' about it.

"I tell them that I don't want them to take our cows. That they have no right to do this. And then they say that yes they do. They say that this was part of the agreement. I ask them what agreement but they just ignore me. They go back to work."

"All right, Duane. You are doing really well now. You are doing a really fine job. What's happening now?"

"They are done with the cow. They are takin' it away. They are cleanin' the table. Everything is real clean. Now they are turning to me. Their eyes are real scary. They are takin' me now. Oh, no! I am on the table! I am on the table! I don't like this! I want to stop this! I don't want to be hypnotized anymore. Bring me back! Mama, tell them to bring me back."

"Duane, it's okay. You can go through this. Just keep

pushing on through..."

Suddenly Mandy spoke.

'That's enough, Doc. You bring my boy back," she said.

Dr Talbot shook his head.

"Not now, Mrs Thompson. Your son is at a critical juncture in his journey. We must bring him through this."

Just then, Dr Talbot heard a metallic click. He turned and saw Mandy standing behind the kitchen table. She was thumbing back the hammer on her .22 magnum pistol.

"You bring that boy back right now," she said sharply, "or next thing you know you're gonna be hypnotizin' angels up at the pearly gates."

"You best listen to her," Hawkins told the doctor.

Talbot frowned.

"This is very irregular," he said.

Mandy narrowed her eyes.

"So is the path this bullet is gonna take through your gullet if you don't bring that boy back."

Dr Horn leaned forward.

"I think Mrs Thompson is right," she told her colleague. "Let's end our session right here."

Talbot shook his head. "Never, in all my years..."

"Just do it," Mandy said.

Dr Talbot turned back to his subject.

"Duane, are you okay?" he asked.

"Yes. I'm just here, on the table. No one is doin' anythin' to me."

"Okay, I'm going to bring you back to the present now. We are going to leave this memory and return. I will talk you through that now..."

Within a few moments, Duane had opened his eyes.

Mandy uncocked her gun and laid it on the kitchen table.

"Are you all right, Duane?" she asked.

Duane's eyes roamed around the room until they rested on his mother.

"Yeah, Mama. I'm fine."

Talbot's voice was tight with anger.

"How do you feel now, Duane?"

"I feel lighter. Like as if a weight has been lifted off me."

"You feel better?"

"Oh, yeah. Listen, Doctor. I know it was hard but I want to go back."

"I think you will have to talk to your mother about that. I refuse to continue until I have an agreement from her that she is not going to –"

"Duane," Mandy said. "I'm sorry, boy. It just pained me to see you all scared like that, all shaken up."

"I know, Mama. But don't you see? I know something, somethin' that's gotta be told. What do you say, Doctor. Will you take me back?"

Talbot turned to Mandy.

"Mrs Thompson, do I have your promise that you will act in a civil manner and not interfere?"

Mandy slid the pistol across the table to Hawkins.

"Here, flyboy. Hold onta this for me, willya?"

Then she turned to Talbot. Her eyes were sharp and defiant.

Talbot nodded, locking eyes with the old woman.

Hawkins shook open the revolver and dumped the snub-nosed bullets out on to the tablecloth.

"That's enough gunplay for one day," the pilot said.

CHAPTER ELEVEN

Duane was lying on the couch again, staring up at the ceiling.

"Are you ready to begin?" Dr Talbot asked.

"I guess so," he said nervously.

Dr Talbot began a series of deep relaxation exercises, using his voice to return Duane to the memory which he had re-experienced that morning.

"We are going to be drifting back in time," Talbot said slowly. "We are going to be returning to that particular night in June of 1979. Let yourself drift back... going deeper and deeper, feeling comfortable and relaxed. You will be able to talk and describe what you see. Can you hear me, Duane?"

"Yes."

"Good. Where are you now?"

"I am on the porch."

"What is happening?"

"Things are happenin' really fast. I see the light. I see the cow being taken up. Now the light is on me. Oh! I'm afraid again...I know I'm not supposed to be..."

"It's all right to be afraid, Duane. Just allow yourself to go through the experience. Tell us what happens next."

"I am in the ship," he said in a shaky voice. "Now I am on the table."

"Yes. Stay with it..."

"They have their hands on me: They are givin' me a medical examination. No! I don't want this! Take me out! I want out of here now!"

"Duane," Dr Talbot said reassuringly, "I want you to listen to me. I understand that you are afraid now. But this is a critical point. You need to continue to push on through."

"But I'm afraid they're gonna cut me, like they did the

cow..."

"Do you see any instruments?"

"Instruments? Like musical instruments?"

"No, I mean medical instruments, knives or lasers or –"

"Wait! Hold on. The examination is over. I am sittin' up on the table now. Everythin' in the spaceship is clean and quiet. I'm okay. I'm gonna be okay. I'm not afraid now. I ask them why they are doin' this. They all ignore me, except for one. He is taller than the rest. He has these large, dark eyes. I almost feel like he's there to calm me down. He is speakin' to me inside my head.

"He says: 'Do you know who we are?'"

"I can hear my voice sayin': 'I guess you are from some other world.'

"I know it's a stupid answer, but he doesn't treat it that way. Instead, he shows me somethin'. He is holdin' it in his hand. It looks sorta like diamond or maybe a rock crystal. But it's pretty big, about the size of a baseball. It seems to have a light of its own. An orange light.

"Then he speaks. 'Here is our home.' I look and see a picture of a small, spinnin' planet. It kinda hangs in the air above the crystal. It's almost like watchin' a movie except that the picture is almost real. I mean, I know it's a picture, but it has depth to it."

"Like a three-dimensional picture?"

"Yeah, like that."

"Good. What's happening now?"

"Now there are a lot of maps and diagrams. Oh, I see. This is a map of the Universe. He is showin' me where the Earth is and now, way over there, that's their planet. It's real far away."

"How far?"

"Real, real far. Thirty-eight light years, he says."

"The name of the planet?"

"Zeta somethin'. I can't get the rest."

"Okay. Just be aware. Now what's happening?"

"He says he is givin' me a lot of information. He says I won't remember it when I get back but that it will come out at the right time. He says that some people on Earth know what he is about to tell me but they are keepin' it a secret.

"He is speakin' in my head now. He says they have been comin' to Earth for about 25,000 years. They have been observin' us and have created human bein's as an experiment.

"He says that they created what we call cro-magnon man. We are a cross between alien and ape-like life forms. Since the early days of our existence, they have made about sixty-five changes to us to get us to the point we're at now. I ask why they would want to do all this and he won't tell me. He just says it's an experiment.

"Up until modern times, they were just observin' us. But when they saw that we had learned how to fly, they got real interested. They began makin' observation flights with their own ships in the 1930s, but didn't have any real contact.

"During World War Two, they became worried about some technological developments takin' place in the southwestern region of the United States. Then, in July of 1947, one of their disks crashed in the desert near Roswell, New Mexico.

"Air Force staff found the wreckage. They also found the bodies of three alien pilots. Everythin' was taken to Los Alamos National Laboratory. Other crashes took place in New Mexico, Arizona and Texas. Bodies and craft were found and examined.

"One of the alien pilots, who crashed in New Mexico in 1949, was found alive. The Air Force took him to Los Alamos where he lived for three years before he died. In that time, he learned to communicate mind-to-mind with humans and dictated *The Yellow Book*, a history of the alien planet. It also contains information about their experiments here on Earth. This document is now kept in the Pentagon in Washington DC. He says this is the biggest secret in the

United States.

"The US Government began communicatin' regularly with the aliens. On April 25, 1964 three space ships landed at Holloman Air Force Base in New Mexico. One of the ships landed and three alien bein's came out. They met for three hours with a team of scientists and military officials.

"That's where they made the agreement. The agreement said they would not interfere with our society as long as we did not try and stop their research efforts. The US Government agreed to create a world-wide cover-up which would keep the public from knowin' anything.

"The aliens also said they needed to have access to cattle and other animals for their experiments. They said they would also be abductin' humans for medical research only. They said they would return them unharmed. The humans would have no conscious memory of the abduction. The aliens agreed to give the Government a list of abductees on a regular basis.

"In exchange, the aliens would give the US Military weapons which would make them the world's only superpower. They also gave them advanced flying technology which would help them maintain their superiority in the air.

"At the end of the Holloman meetin', there was a hostage exchange as a pledge that each side would keep its agreement. One of our pilots went with them. They left behind a pilot named Krill, who died a few years later.

"They started takin' the animals and the people right after that. But the cover-up worked real well. Anyone who said they saw a UFO was made to look like a fool.

"The light in the crystal is changin' now. He is showing me somethin' else. Oh, now I understand... he say that there are plenty of other bein's from other planets in the Universe who are visitin' us, there have been maybe nine different –"

Just then, they heard the sound of shattering glass.

Hawkins turned and saw something rolling across the

kitchen floor, spewing a cloud of pungent smoke. It was tear gas. Hawkins went down on all fours, pulling Mandy with him. He headed for the back door.

"Duane!" the old woman shouted.

But there was no answer from the back of the room. Just a raspy chorus of coughs and the heavy sound of furniture being knocked over.

Hawkins crawled down the narrow hallway and shoved his shoulder against the back door. He tumbled out on to the ground, dragging Mandy with him. They lay there, gasping for air. A moment later, Duane, Dr Horn and Dr Talbot came stumbling out behind them.

As Hawkins wiped the tears from his eyes, he saw the unmarked panel vans, tucked back in the hills. Then the Delta Force guards were all around them, pulling them to their feet and dragging them toward the vehicles.

Hawkins threw a glance back in Mandy's direction. She was kicking wildly with her snakeskin boots and screeching like a banshee. Farther back, in a fog of tear gas, he saw a dozen burly men in camouflage fatigues, wresting the others to the ground. For a second, he caught glimpse of Duane Thompson's face. He was kneeling, with the guards all around him. His eyes were closed and he was vomiting on to the ground.

The next thing he knew, Hawkins was face-down on the metal floor of the van. He felt his shoulders joints pop as his arms were twisted behind him. A pair of steel handcuffs bit into his wrists. Then he felt a burning sensation in the right thigh. He turned his head to the side and saw one of the guards injecting him with a large hypodermic needle. A second later, everything went black.

Afterword

Hawkins never saw any of the others again. When he woke up, he was informed by an unfriendly guard that he had been shipped to Nellis Air Force Base, just north of Las Vegas. Hawkins fully expected to be imprisoned, maybe even executed.

But he was not. He was simply given his retirement paperwork and told to keep his mouth shut. The stone-faced officer who debriefed him mentioned that Hawkins should advise his sister to avoid long-distance driving with her two young daughters because the roadways are dangerous and accidents can happen. Today, the research teams in Area 51 are still working on a wide array of advanced technology, developing aircraft and weapons systems which seem to be borrowed from the distant future. The public only learns about these top-secret projects through small cracks which appear in the security system.

Major Hawkins and Dr Horn tried to circumvent that system and were immediately banished from 'Dreamland'. What marvels might they have seen if they had managed to stay with the program for just a few more weeks?

Perhaps someday the Government files will be opened and the truth about the research efforts inside Area 51 will be released. Until then, we can only guess at what mysteries are unfolding, each night, in the arid skies over the Nevada desert.

As for the ones who remained on the project – Dr Mendelssohn, Colonel Sheridan and Major Comstock – we can only suppose that they continued in their struggle to gain a working knowledge of the technological marvels that had been placed in their care.

Dr Horn's name has disappeared from the scientific community. Following her brief stint in Area 51, she did not resurface in any teaching, administrative or research capacity.

Following the raid on the ranch, Mandy Thompson was held for a few hours at the local Sheriff's office. She was charged with breaking the nose of one of the Delta Force guards but was later released and returned to live a quiet life on her ranch outside Rachel. Curiously enough, the cattle mutilations stopped.

Duane Thompson actually benefited from Dr Talbot's brief but intense sessions. Once the shock and confusion of the Delta Force incident passed, his health improved and his chronic headaches disappeared.

As for Hawkins, he suddenly found himself retired and restless. After his discharge, he returned to his sister's house in Texas, where he spent a few weeks helping her paint and wallpaper her daughter's room.

As summer edged into autumn, he joined the silent army of fisherman and began single-mindedly to pursue his life-long interest in fly fishing. Eventually, he bought a twin-engined plane and ran a part-time business transporting fisherman up and down the spine of the Rocky Mountains.

In August of 1995, Hawkins's sister received word that his bush plane had crashed on the shores of a remote lake in the Canadian wilderness. His body was never found.

GLOSSARY

ABDUCTEES
People who report that they have been abducted
by aliens. Their testimony is sometimes available
only through hypnotic regression.

ANIMAL MUTILATION
Unexplained mutilations of animals are a world-
wide phenomenon, often associated with the
sightings of what witnesses believe to be
extraterrestrial spacecraft.

AREA 51
Top-secret military installation located in the
Nevada desert which serves as a testing ground
for the US Military's most advanced aircraft and
weapons systems.

BACK-ENGINEERING
Scientists use this term to describe the process of
tearing something apart in order to discover how
it works.

CIA (CENTRAL INTELLIGENCE AGENCY)
US agency charged with protecting the US from
hostile foreign countries through a variety of
clandestine activities. Works to maintain the
secrecy of matters which are vital to national
security.

DELTA FORCE
An elite, non-military cadre of combat veterans

allegedly charged with guarding captured alien spacecraft.

DISINFORMATION
A Government tactic for concealing information which involves mixing truth and fiction in such a way that it is difficult to determine the actual facts.

EBE (EXTRATERRESTRIAL BIOLOGICAL ENTITIES)
Term used to describe visitors from other planets in what appear to be Government documents. The authenticity of these documents has not been completely established. Officially, the Government denies any knowledge of contact with EBEs.

ELEMENT 115
The super-heavy element not found on this planet which some researchers believe could be used to power a spacecraft capable of long-distance space travel.

HOLLOMAN LANDING
Some writers believe US officials met with alien visitors in April 1964 at Holloman Air Force Base in New Mexico, and forged a top-secret agreement which formally established diplomatic relations between the United States and the EBEs. The Government denies that this ever happened.

H-PAC (HUMAN-PILOTED ALIEN CRAFT)
Military term which test pilots allegedly use to refer to captured alien spacecraft which human pilots are learning to fly.

HYPNOTIC REGRESSION

A technique which allows the hypnotist to retrieve information from the patient's subconscious mind which may not have been previously available. The actual credibility of these 'memories' is a subject of intense debate.

NASA (NATIONAL AERONAUTIC AND SPACE ADMINISTRATION)

The US agency specializing in aerial flight and space travel.

NELLIS AIR FORCE BASE

Air Force installation north of Las Vegas.

PROJECT GALILEO

A reputed top-secret Government project aimed at back-engineering and flying captured spacecraft.

POST TRAUMATIC STRESS SYNDROME

A psychological disorder which afflicts people who have undergone a experience so traumatic that their normal means of coping becomes disabled. Survivors of airline crashes and veterans of wars are among those effected by this malady.

ROSWELL CRASH

An alleged crash of a spaceship in the New Mexico desert in 1949. The Government says it did not happen.

S-4

The top secret installation within Area 51 where some witnesses say the US stored and flew alien spacecraft.

Biographies

This story is a fictional account of a true-life mystery. Before you look at the facts and make up your own mind, here is a brief biography of the characters:

MAJOR CHARLIE COMSTOCK
(FICTIONAL)

Air Force test pilot assigned to Area 51. In addition to being a skilful pilot, Comstock holds a degree in Aeronautical Design from the Air Force Academy.

MAJOR DANIEL HAWKINS
(FICTIONAL)

Highly decorated Air Force test pilot assigned to Project Galileo in Area 51. Degree in Aeronautical Design from the Air Force Academy. Fly fishing enthusiast.

DOCTOR BARBARA HORN
(FICTIONAL)

Part of the research team formed to back-engineer alien craft at S-4. Holds a PhD in Physics from California Technical Institute.

DOCTOR HERBERT MENDELSSOHN
(FICTIONAL)

Head of the scientific research team at S-4. Holds a PhD in Physics from Harvard.

LIEUTENANT COLONEL ROBERT SHERIDAN
(FICTIONAL)

Career Air Force officer, Galileo Project Director
assigned to Area 51.

DOCTOR GREGORY TALBOT
(FICTIONAL)

Psychiatrist in private practice in Los Angeles,
California who uses hypnotic regression as a
primary therapeutic technique.

DUANE THOMPSON
(FICTIONAL)

Rancher's son who has lived all his life in the
vicinity of Rachel, Nevada. Talented artist.

MANDY THOMPSON
(FICTIONAL)

Owner of the the Circle S Ranch in Rachel,
Nevada. Mother of Duane. Desert recluse
and cattle rancher.

CLASSIFIED FILES

Is it possible that the US Government has alien spacecraft in its possession?
Did the military receive these ships as part of a 'technology exchange' with beings from a distant planet? And is it possible that our leaders could keep a secret this powerful from the public for so long?

To find the answers, let's piece together the facts as we know them.

AREA 51

The secret air base at Area 51 - fact or fiction?

Although the Government will not admit that it exists, Area 51 is a real place. Over the years, the top-secret base has gone by many names – 'Dreamland,' 'The Ranch', 'the Funny Farm' – but whatever it has been called, it has always been shrouded in the deepest secrecy.

The US Central Intelligence Agency (CIA), with help from Lockheed Aircraft founder Kelly Johnson, picked the spot for the base back in the early 1950s. A small facility, accessible only by air, was built there in 1955 and operated under the direct control of the CIA.

According to George Knapp, a US journalist who has been working on the Area 51 story for more than ten years, this base has functioned as a top-secret test site for the Government's most advanced aircraft and weapons technology: the U-2, SR-71, Stealth fighter, Stealth bomber and even the 'Star Wars' beam weaponry were developed and tested there.

Russian satellite photos show a grid of buildings and two very long runways on the dry bed of Groom Lake. Civilian watchdog operations, like the Area 51 Research Centre, have used cameras equipped with powerful telephoto lenses to take photos of the facility.

Because the area is in a remote corner of the Nevada desert, protected by mountain ranges on all sides, it would seem to be a perfect location for top-secret operations.

Farther west of Groom Lake, across one more mountain range, the maps show a dry lake bed called Papoose Lake. There, in camouflaged hangars built into the mountainside, some observers believe alien spacecraft are stored and tested. The existence of the Papoose Lake facility (sometimes called S-4) has never been openly acknowledged.

Over the years, the military has taken great care to ensure that unauthorized persons are kept in the dark about what goes on in Area 51. The projects undertaken there are among those funded by a 35-billion-dollar 'black budget' which even the highest-ranking members of Congress are not permitted to review.

Although we can establish that many clandestine programs have been conducted in Area 51, the only way we can come close to confirming the alien spacecraft story is through the testimony of individuals who have come forward in the last ten years to tell of their experiences at the air base.

THE LAZAR STORY

The most prominent witness to the Area 51 story
is a US scientist named Bob Lazar. Lazar claims
to have been part of a research effort to back-
engineer alien spacecraft in Area 51 during a six-
month period in 1988-89. Lazar's story has
raised a firestorm of controversy. Some dismiss
him as a fake, others insist that he holds the key
to what could be the story of the century.

But people like journalist George Knapp insist
that even if you take Bob Lazar out of the
picture, you have still got a story, one which is
supported by the corroborating testimony of
dozens of people who have worked in the secret
military base.

George Knapp is one of the several writers
who have conducted an exhaustive search for
people who might be able to confirm the details
of Lazar's fantastic story. What Knapp and others
have uncovered is perhaps one of the most
fascinating tales of modern time.

 Let's take a look at Bob Lazar's claims and the testimony of others in the Area 51 drama.

Lazar says he was hired in 1988 to work on
Project Galileo – the Government project to back-
engineer and test fly the alien craft stored at S-4.
He believes he was recommended for the job by
Edward Teller, 'the father' of the H-bomb, who
met Lazar briefly a few years before.

Lazar says that, before being hired to work at S-4, he worked at the Los Alamos National Laboratory in New Mexico. He claims to have a degree in Electronic Technology from California Technical Institute and a degree in Physics from Massachusetts Institute of Technology.

 Despite exhaustive efforts by several researchers, no one has been able to verify this conclusively. Lazar says that his records were removed by the Government in an effort to discredit him.

The Lazar story has more twists and turns than a cheap mystery novel and challenges the determination of even the most ardent believers. The problem is further complicated by the fact that Lazar does not seem to care whether anyone believes him or not. He created a sensation in October, 1989 when he appeared on George Knapp's evening show on KLAS-TV in Las Vegas. He discussed his work at the base as well as the troubled personal times he experienced after he was forced out of the Project. Here is his story:

In a six-month period, Lazar says he visited S-4 on four occasions. He was taken there under heavy supervision, given a specific task, then returned to Las Vegas the same day.

On his first visit, Lazar says he was taken out to S-4, shown the disks and then put to work. The technical description of the propulsion system in Chapter Four is taken directly from Lazar's video-taped testimony.

Even though he has produced a video which explains the workings of the system in terms an ordinary person can understand, Lazar has been reluctant to release complete details about the propulsion system.

"The entire concept I have no problem bringing forth," he told Knapp, *"but the inner workings and the details I still believe should remain classified. You have to understand that the reason these systems are being kept quiet is that everything is being looked at from a weapons point of view. I have no intention, and never have had, of releasing precisely how the thing works."*

Lazar noted that the energy which lies dormant in element 115 could be used to make a very powerful bomb. The military has gone to great lengths to make sure that this material does not fall into the hands of individuals or governments who might use the power of this *'superbomb'* as a way of persuading others to do their bidding.

While the creation of a weapon from element 115 is only a proposal, Lazar insists that the use of the superheavy material as an antigravity fuel *has* been successfully tested by the research teams out at S-4.

Lazar says the flight tests were conducted very conservatively and that he is sure none of the craft left the Earth's atmosphere during his time in Area 51. The night the craft was scheduled to conduct a high-performance test flight, Lazar committed a glaring indiscretion: he couldn't contain his excitement about the project. He had to tell someone. He took his wife and two friends to a mountain top about twenty-five kilometres away, where they set up a telescope. There they watched some strangely lit objects *'jump'* across the sky over S-4. Lazar surmised that these were experimental anti-gravity flights with the alien craft.

They returned the following week and videotaped further flights. Then, on the evening of April 6, they were caught. Security guards arrested Lazar. He was interrogated and threatened. They reminded him of the oaths he had signed. Lazar fully expected to be punished. But he was not. He was simply discharged from the Project and told to keep quiet.

It was then that Lazar approached George Knapp and went public with his story. The scientist said he felt that people should know about the clandestine activities. He also stated that he felt going public would be his best protection against Government reprisals. He reasoned that if he could keep himself in the public spotlight, the Government would be reluctant to harm him.

Lazar's astonishing account has become one of the most hotly-debated topics in ufology. During the televised interviews, Lazar further intrigued his listeners by describing briefing papers he read during his brief stay at S-4. Although he could not attest to the truth of the documents, he reported that these briefs made the startling claim that aliens from the distant planet Zeta Reticulli had been visiting the Earth for tens of thousands of years. According to the briefings, the aliens had actually created human beings through sixty five genetic corrections made over the course of our evolution. Lazar says he got the impression that the Earth is a type of zoo and that all humans are subjects in a huge, on-going experiment.

According to the briefing papers, the alien spacecraft were obtained through an interchange of technology between alien beings and scientists. He said aliens worked in underground facilities at S-4 up until 1979 when there was a confrontation because of a misunderstanding between an alien and one of the security guards. One of the aliens killed several of the security personnel – delivering fatal head wounds – and left the facility. That was the end of the alien cooperation with researchers, although the craft were left behind for study.

While Lazar is careful to point out that he cannot prove that any of the documents he read were factual, he says that the technical data he worked with was clearly accurate. So perhaps all the data he was given was truthful. On the other hand, Lazar admits that the briefing papers could have been part of a Government disinformation plan to confuse or mislead him. Nonetheless, Lazar insists that the alien hardware was no illusion.

"I am telling the truth," Lazar told Knapp, *"I have tried to prove that. What's going on up there could be the most important event in history. You're talking about physical contact with and proof from another system – another planet, another intelligence. That's got to be the biggest event in history – period."*

OTHER WITNESSES

Knapp says that since the Lazar's initial broadcast, more than fifty witnesses have come forward to confirm the scientist's story. Knapp says he has learned that it was common knowledge among Area 51 employees that extraterrestrial craft were stored at the Nevada test site.

A former Air Force radar operator who worked at the base told Knapp that he and his companions watched unusual objects flying over the Groom Range for five successive nights. According to their radar equipment, the objects moved at a rate of over 11,000 kilometres per hour, stopped in mid-air, then zoomed off in another direction. When he reported his findings to his superiors, they told him that what he had witnessed had *"never happened."*

A further testimony comes from former CIA officer Marion Williams. He claimed *"the Earth was being visited by nonhuman intelligent species, that the American Government researchers are busy conducting genetic studies of intact alien corpses recovered from crashed alien spacecraft, and that design principles from the saucers have been utilized in the Stealth bomber."*

Is There Anybody Out There?

Accounts of visitors from another world have been published since biblical times and have led to endless speculation about the actual nature of these visitations.

But, as author Whitley Strieber points out, our speculation doesn't have to be random, it can be careful and directed.

Here are some suggestions he offers:

"The visitors could be:

from another planet or planets.

from Earth, but so different from us that we have not hitherto understood that they are even real.

from another aspect of space-time, in effect another dimension.

from this dimension in space but not in time. We cannot assume that time travel is out of the question.

from within us. I suppose the idea that the gods we create would turn out to be real because we created them has a certain ironic appeal to a modern intellectual.

a side effect of a natural phenomenon.
    Perhaps there are certain electromagnetic
anomalies that trip a certain hallucinatory wire
in the mind, causing many different people to
have experiences so similar as to seem to be the
result of encounters with the same physical
phenomenon.

an aspect of the human species. We have a
    very ancient tradition of afterlife. Maybe
we do have an afterlife, but not quite in the way
the tradition suggests. Maybe you and I are
larvae, and the 'visitors' are human beings in the
mature form. Certainly, we are consuming our
planet's resources with at least the avidity of
caterpillars on a shrub."

Ultimately, the fate of all the life forms on the
planet may hinge upon how we address this
critical question. As Strieber points out, our
present practice of ruthlessly consuming the
planet's resources will not sustain us into the
future. Our species must radically alter its
evolution if we, and the other beings we share
the planet with, are to survive.

Perhaps now is the time to open the secret
files and deliver this information into the hands
of the common person. Maybe this way, all
Earthlings can combine their hopes and fears and
begin a dialogue with our far-flung neighbours.
Maybe then we can take the first steps toward
understanding our place in the Cosmos.

CLASSIFIED

Reader, your brief is to be on the alert for the following spine-tingling books.